Dear Reader,

I'm embarrassed to say this story began with one simple idea. I wanted a love scene under a waterfall.

I mentioned this to my Romance Book Club members and one of them, who'd just returned from a trip, said, "There are plenty of waterfalls in Hawaii."

At the time, I'd just finished writing *Primal Calling,* set in the coldest part of Alaska, and I was ready for some sunny tropical weather. How simple, right? But I hope I made up for it with my characters. A discussion at book club around that time was about a breast cancer survivor, and immediately a character started forming in my mind.

The heroine—a breast cancer survivor—and the hero, an army captain with PTSD, are definitely dark subjects and not necessarily conducive to romance. But then, if there's anything I believe in, it's the power of love. Love for self, love for family members and even love for a lonely man haunted by guilt. Love can make you a better person, love can give you the strength to overcome adversity, and love can heal a scarred soul. I hope you enjoy Kristen's and Luke's struggles to love each other and let that love heal what was once broken.

I so enjoy hearing from readers. You can reach me through my website, www.jillianburns.com, and while you're there check out my latest news and future releases.

Jillian Burns

Jillian Burns

ONCE A HERO...

TORONTO NEW YORK LONDON
AMSTERDAM PARIS SYDNEY HAMBURG
STOCKHOLM ATHENS TOKYO MILAN MADRID
PRAGUE WARSAW BUDAPEST AUCKLAND

Recycling programs
for this product may
not exist in your area.

ISBN-13: 978-0-373-79674-8

ONCE A HERO...

ABOUT THE AUTHOR

Jillian Burns has always read romance, and spent her teens immersed in the worlds of Jane Eyre and Elizabeth Bennett. She lives in Texas with her husband of twenty years and their three active kids. Jillian likes to think her emotional nature—sometimes referred to as *moodiness*—has found the perfect outlet in writing stories filled with passion and romance. She believes romance novels have the power to change lives with their message of eternal love and hope.

Books by Jillian Burns

HARLEQUIN BLAZE
466—LET IT RIDE
572—SEDUCE AND RESCUE
602—PRIMAL CALLING

To get the inside scoop on Harlequin Blaze and its talented writers, be sure to check out blazeauthors.com.

All backlist available in ebook. Don't miss any of our special offers. Write to us at the following address for information on our newest releases.

Harlequin Reader Service
U.S.: 3010 Walden Ave., P.O. Box 1325, Buffalo, NY 14269
Canadian: P.O. Box 609, Fort Erie, Ont. L2A 5X3

This book is dedicated to all U.S. service members
with Post-Traumatic Stress Syndrome.
You are not alone and your country
owes you a debt of gratitude.

Acknowledgments

This story wouldn't have happened without
my wonderful Romance Book Club friends
Deb, Kelley and Arline!

I owe my SCUBA information to my goddaughter,
Jennifer, my sanity to my two critique partners
extraordinaire, Pam and Linda, and my clean
laundry to my heroic husband, who never complains
about my deadline craziness. I also need to
express deep gratitude to my editor, Kathryn.

1

"CALL 9-1-1!" KRISTEN TURNER yelled at the gathering crowd.

A piercing scream wasn't all that unusual at the Tradewinds Bar and Grill late at night, except this scream had come from a gray-haired woman in a flowered muumuu, and the paunchy older gentleman beside her was flailing about, his face as red-and-purple-mottled as a Maui sunset.

The man was choking.

Kristen knew how to do the Heimlich—in theory—but getting her arms around this nice, but rather barrel-chested man, might be tough.

Before she could move behind him, a tall, dark-haired man swooped in, wrapped his long, muscular arms around the man and administered the Heimlich so perfectly, the chunk of BBQ chicken wing flew out of the older man's throat and landed on the table.

The crowd applauded and whistled, but the mystery

hero slowly lowered the older man to the floor and put his ear to the man's chest.

The older man's eyes were closed and the mystery man began performing CPR on him. He gave four harsh pumps to the man's chest, and then held the man's nose shut and breathed into his mouth a couple of times. Another four strong pushes on the chest, and another set of mouth-to-mouths.

Oblivious to the crowd around him, the guy worked tirelessly. Kristen could see beads of sweat rolling down his temple as he put everything he had into saving the other man's life.

The wail of sirens approached and then paramedics elbowed their way through the crowd and knelt beside the fallen man. But just as they got out their equipment, the mystery hero stopped pumping and the older man drew in a quick breath and opened his eyes. The wife was hysterical as she hugged her husband. One of the paramedics eased her away while the other examined her husband.

They put on a blood-pressure cuff and stuck some round pads, attached to wires, on his chest and started an IV, but...the old man was already conscious and talking. If it hadn't been for the mystery man this night might have turned out quite differently.

Hairs on Kristen's arms stood up and the goose bumps made her shiver.

The wife asked about the mystery man, wanted to

thank him, and everyone looked around, but he'd disappeared.

The older gentleman was rolled away on a gurney, his wife trotting alongside him, holding his hand, and the rest of the customers went back to their tables and drinks. The Beach Boys' "Surfin' Safari" boomed through the speakers, and some tables raised their glasses in a toast to the "stranger who saved the day."

Rubbing her arms, Kristen leaned in the doorway and stared after the ambulance as it drove away. Then she scanned the road both ways and the area all around the Tradewinds. But there was no sign of the mystery man, as she'd begun thinking of him. Who did that kind of thing in this day and age? Didn't the guy want his fifteen minutes of fame?

It seemed not. The mystery man must subscribe to the comic-book code of life, where, once a hero saves the day, he flies off into the night and no one ever knows his true identity.

With a shout, Luke shot up from his bed, blinking in the darkness until he found the green glow of the clock. 1:00 a.m. He pressed his palms to his eyes and swiped his hands through his sweat-soaked hair.

Another damned nightmare.

So much for getting any more sleep tonight.

Luke got out of bed, dropped to his stomach and counted out fifty push-ups. Then he rolled to his back, laced his fingers behind his head and did fifty

Once a Hero...

crunches. After that, fifty lunges. But the images from his nightmare didn't go away.

After a hot shower, he stepped into his jeans and padded out to the kitchen. He opened the fridge, grabbed the white carton of leftover sesame chicken and the chopsticks, and carried them out of the condo. He rode the elevator down and crossed Kihei Road to a picnic table on Kamaole Beach.

The ocean breeze cooled his dampened face and body, and the constant crash of the waves calmed his thoughts. His buddy John, back at Fort Sam Houston, had been half-right. Maui was peaceful, all right. The air here was soft, and perfumed with the sweet fragrance of tropical flowers. The palm trees swayed, and the ocean sparkled with moonlight. But the calm and quiet hadn't stopped the nightmares.

Not yet, anyway.

He'd only been here a few days. John had generously lent him the use of his condo for the rest of Luke's leave. Surely three more weeks of living on this island paradise would be enough to get his head straight.

A dog whined and Luke glanced in the direction of the sound. A scruffy mutt the size of a shepherd sat on his haunches staring at him. "What are you looking at?"

As if he'd understood perfectly, the dog made a point of glancing down at Luke's Chinese food, and his tongue came out and licked his muzzle.

Aah. The guy was hungry. Okay, boy. Luke really didn't want the rest. He set the carton down a few feet in front of him and before he'd even straightened up, the dog had lapped up what was left. He licked the container clean and then lay down with a loud sigh.

Luke bent down to retrieve the carton, turned to pitch it into the trash receptacle and stopped midpitch. Standing across the grassy slope, under the streetlight was a young woman, small and slim and wearing a white T-shirt and cutoffs. She tugged off her helmet and Luke's heart literally jumped.

It was the girl, the waitress from the bar tonight. Had she followed him?

She crouched down to chain her bike to the rack, straightened and toed off her sneakers and then skipped down to the surf.

Her straight blond hair lifted in the gentle wind and Luke caught his breath when she raised her face and arms to the full moon, blew it a kiss and then twirled. Her smile put the moon's glow to shame.

Before he could fully admire her slim legs she ran into the ocean. He jumped up to stop her, thinking she was crazy or suicidal. Who did that at two-thirty in the morning? But she darted back up to dry land as the waves crashed around her.

Frolicking. There was no other word for it. She was frolicking in the moonlit sea. Her laughter carried to him across the breeze and made his chest tighten. Such joy. If only she could bottle that up, he'd buy a case.

What was she doing? Was dancing in the ocean her own personal remedy for insomnia?

Maybe he was still dreaming. Wouldn't that be cool? To be having this kind of dream and be getting a good night's sleep while he was at it?

Not possible. His psyche could never conjure up someone so unusual. He held still, cloaked in the darkness of the tree cover, wondering what she'd do next.

As she headed back toward her bike, he swallowed and hoped she wouldn't see him. But she was still twenty yards or more away and walked past without noticing him. Reaching her bike, she unlocked the chain, and then walked it across the street and into the foyer of his condo building.

They were neighbors?

Luke got up and headed over to the condo. The dog trotted after him and tried to slip inside the lobby door as Luke opened it.

"Hold on there, mutt." Luke closed the door with both of them still outside. But under the bright lobby lights shining through the glass Luke saw what looked like blood, still wet, all over the dog's left side. "What the..." He squatted to get a closer look and the dog sat, panting up at him trustingly.

Luke's shoulders slumped. The mutt had been scraped by something. A car, a boulder, something rough. He checked for broken ribs and didn't feel any, but the dog could have internal injuries. Still, even if he knew where a vet's office was, it probably wouldn't be open at two-thirty in the morning. There were gauze and bandages in the condo....

He let out an audible sigh, opened the door and ushered the dog inside the lobby and up the elevator to his condo.

He'd take him to a vet first thing tomorrow.

THE FOLLOWING EVENING, Luke lay in bed, staring at the rattan dresser across the bedroom. How did they get that wood to curlicue like that? And was the cane naturally that color or was that painted?

Nice. He'd been reduced to wondering about furniture making.

Close your eyes, Andrews. Relax. Deep breaths...

Forget it. He flipped back the sheets, swung his legs off the mattress and dropped to the floor for his usual workout.

The mutt, now bathed and bandaged, lifted his head, but otherwise remained lying on the floor at the foot of the bed.

The vet had said the dog was a shepherd mix, x-rayed it for internal injuries and found none. But he hadn't had room to board the stray. The vet prescribed a bottle of antibiotics and directions to the nearest shelter ten miles away in Puunene. Luke planned to drop him off there in a couple of days, after the mutt healed a little more.

Tomorrow he'd have to get some dog food and some more bandages. In the meantime, no sense wasting a 60" flat screen and nine hundred channels....

LUKE JERKED AWAKE ON a choked-off shout. Geez. He'd fallen asleep in the club chair in the living room. The dog whined and stuck his cold nose under Luke's hand. Bleary-eyed, he found the TV remote, switched off the infomercial, then stumbled to the bathroom and splashed water on his face. The dream had been different this time. Bloodier.

Feeling nauseated, he avoided the mirror above the sink and made his way to the balcony. He opened the sliding glass door and stepped out into a salty sea breeze and the reassuring sound of crashing waves.

After a couple of deep gulps of air, he leaned his forearms on the railing and stared into the night sky. There was a bottle of over-the-counter sleeping pills in the bathroom medicine cabinet. Maybe he should try one. But he should be able to deal with this without resorting to medication, damn it.

Give it time, Andrews. The advice had come from John, along with the key to his condo. And John had studied psychotherapy before switching to orthopedics.

This *was* only Luke's fourth day here.

From the corner of his eye, he caught sight of that same blonde he'd seen last night pedaling her bike southbound on Kihei Road. He turned his wrist and checked his watch. Two-thirty. Again.

She dismounted and chained her bike to the rack just as she'd done the night before. She wore the same outfit, too. She turned away and headed down to the surf. As she had the night before, the blonde lifted her face and arms to the moon. Was she some sort of new-age moon worshipper?

After playing in the surf awhile she went back to her bike and walked it to the condo. Just before she entered the foyer she looked up. Without thinking, he stepped back into the shadowed doorway.

Luke held his breath. *What are you doing, Andrews, you moron?* So what if she knew he'd been watching her?

Should he step out to the balcony and act as if he'd just gone back inside to get something? Smile and wave as if this were just a normal meeting? But he couldn't force his lips to curve upward. It was almost as if he'd forgotten how to smile. But it turned out it didn't matter. When he braved the balcony again, she was gone.

KRISTEN TURNER HURRIED into the tiny bathroom of the Tradewinds Bar and Grill, wiggled out of her grass skirt and toed off her high heels.

Amy followed her in, plunked her makeup bag next to the sink and started touching up her lipstick in the mirror. "You sure are in a hurry."

Kristen froze in the act of unzipping her backpack and shrugged. "I'm just ready to get home and put my feet up."

With Amy's raised brows and pursed lips, she didn't have to say the word *Riiiight* out loud.

But Kristen chose to ignore her. She pulled her shorts and sneakers from her backpack and stuffed the skirt and high heels in.

"You really think you'll see him again tonight?"

Amy turned away from the mirror and waggled her brows. "Captain Mysterious?"

Kristen grinned as she tied her shoelaces. The name the bar patrons had given him had stuck and the story had spread among the staff who hadn't been working that night.

She'd barely caught a glimpse of him on the balcony, and had half convinced herself she'd conjured him up from wishful thinking. She couldn't believe her hero from the other night lived in her building. But she'd have recognized that angled jaw and those biceps below his white T-shirt sleeves anywhere.

"*If* it's him, he probably thinks I'm some psych-ward patient if he saw me in my 'celebrate life' moment."

"Nah, I bet he's into you. He probably noticed you that night he was here. Why else would he be waiting on his balcony at that time of night?"

"Uh, 'cause he's a serial killer stalking his next victim? Or a vampire? Or maybe he's a werewolf watching for the full moon?"

Amy giggled as she rummaged around in her voluminous purse and pulled out a hairbrush. "Your own personal Edward or Jacob, huh? Which does he have? Edward's smoldering passion, or Jacob's rock-hard abs?"

Kristen felt a tiny flurry in her stomach picturing the mystery man. "Both." The word came out kind of breathy and Amy gave her a sharp look.

"Both? Good grief, no wonder you're all gaga over him."

"I'm not gaga. I just thought he was…intriguing. Leaving like that before he could be thanked."

Amy shrugged. "Maybe he was afraid of a lawsuit. You know what they say. No good deed goes unpunished."

"Wow. Cynical much?" Kristen worried about her friend's hard-edged attitude toward life. "What are you getting all fixed up for?"

Turning back to the mirror, Amy ran the brush through her long red curls. Kristen's self-esteem took a hit every time she compared her own straight ordinary hair to those luscious red curls.

"Didn't you say Kekoa mentioned he might drop by sometime?" Amy dropped the question so offhandedly that Kristen knew it wasn't a casual inquiry.

"The guy who drives the boat I use? He might have mentioned he liked that Sneaky Tiki you made him last time he came in to bring me his new brochures. But we have to be at the dive site by seven to beat all the tour boats. I doubt he'll show up now."

Amy visibly deflated, her mouth turned down. "Oh." She dropped her brush back into her purse.

"You like him!" Kristen shoved Amy's shoulder with her own.

Amy spun to face Kristen. "What's not to like with that smooth, dark skin and those intelligent black eyes? And his broad chest and shoulders look like he could row a girl all the way to the Big Island if he had to. Don't you think he's the sexiest guy you ever met? You gotta invite me on a dive, Kris."

Kristen winced, hating to turn her friend down. "You know I'd love to, but, Kekoa isn't just my boat driver, he's my dive partner, too."

"Please?" Amy begged. "I promise not to distract him. I've been dying to see where you dive, anyway. And, hey, maybe you could invite Captain Mysterious along. I'll bring my famous triple-berry muffins."

"Okay, okay." Kristen chuckled, holding her hands up in surrender. "I'll ask Kekoa. Maybe we could set something up for next week sometime."

Amy hugged Kristen. "Thanks, girlfriend. All I want is a chance."

"You might need more than that. Kekoa's not easy to get to know."

"We'll see." Amy's gaze slipped away and her expression softened. "He's got a lot of passion lurking beneath the surface. I can tell."

"Kekoa?" Kristen didn't see it, but...whatever. "If you say so. I'm off tomorrow, so I'll text you if it's Monday," she said as she left the restroom, waved to her boss and headed for her bike.

It was barely a third of a mile from the Tradewinds to her condo on South Kihei Road and she was at her building before she'd even thought about what she might say if she saw the stranger again. But then again, what kind of conversation could she have yelling up at him on his balcony?

Wanting to soak her aching feet in the warm water before heading inside, she braked at the bike rack, swung her leg over the bike, took off her helmet and attached it to a handlebar.

After going knee-deep in the surf and wiggling her toes into the soft sand, she headed back up to her bike. A dog barking to her right made her catch her breath and jump. Her gaze shot to a tan shepherd mix running toward her and the tall shadow following the dog.

Her heart pumped stronger for one beat before she recognized it was him. Captain Mysterious.

The dog reached her side and she hunkered down to let him smell her hand. He nuzzled into her chest and almost knocked her over. Catching herself with her hands behind her, she laughed as the dog tried to lick her face.

"Hey, mutt." The dark stranger grabbed the dog and held him away so she could get to her feet. "Sorry about that."

Kristen stood, wiping her hands on her shorts. "No worries. He's sweet." She smiled and looked the man in the eyes. She had to lift her gaze way up. Her five-foot-two height seemed even more petite against his six-foot frame.

He dropped his gaze and wrestled the dog into sitting. "He's not mine."

She hesitated. "Oh." She stood there a second as

he looked anywhere but at her. Was that a signal for *go away?* Or was he just shy? Is that why he'd ducked back inside his condo last night? Finally, she stuck out her right hand. "I'm Kristen Turner."

He cleared his throat and finally met her gaze. Kristen's pulse fluttered. His eyes. Their deep brown color seemed to bear all the emotions his face refused to acknowledge. Despair. Dismissal. And hope. The despair drew her. The dismissal challenged her. And the hope cinched the deal.

"Luke Andrews." He let go of the dog, who he'd been gently petting, and slid his hand into hers. Heat. Energy. Smooth skin. Long, slim fingers. She held on, not wanting to let whatever was passing between their hands go just yet.

He pulled his hand away.

Did he remember her from the other night? Was that why he was acting so on edge? Only one way to find out.

"I just got off work. I'm a cocktail waitress at the Tradewinds down the road. I...saw you save that man the other night."

He glanced up at her with apprehension lining his forehead.

"Don't worry. I'm not going to give away your secret identity."

He tilted his head, looking confused.

She waved a hand. "You know, the whole save a life and then disappear thing?"

"Oh." He stuck his hands in his back pockets and dropped his gaze to the grass, studying it intently.

"Anyway, if you come back sometime, my manager would love to comp you a meal. We have great chicken wings." She smiled. "And they're usually safe to eat."

One dark brow rose at that, but at least he wasn't staring at the grass anymore. "Maybe I'll try it sometime."

"So, you work nights, too?"

She thought she heard a grunt as he spun at the waist to locate his dog, who'd trotted down to the beach and was sniffing at something in the sand. "You might say that. But I'm on vacation right now."

"Oh." She nodded and the nodding turned into a slow head bobbing. Her gaze moved out to the ocean. Was he trying to be mysterious? Or was he trying to get her to leave him alone? "Well, I guess I should leave you to—"

"I've only been here a few days, so... Can you recommend any sights I shouldn't miss?"

"Well, there's the Maui Ocean Center."

He nodded. "Okay."

"And Mount Haleakala. It's over ten thousand feet."

"Sounds ambitious."

She grinned. "And, of course, the humpbacks."

"Excuse me?"

"The whales. You're lucky to be here in February. Their favorite breeding ground is just off the coast of Maui this time of year."

"Really?"

"Yeah, there're several cruises that take tourists out to see them."

"Humpbacks."

"Of course, you'd have to put on your thick glasses and slump your shoulders for that." She grinned.

His brows drew together and he blinked.

Her smile slowly faded. "You know, the superhero? When he wore his glasses he was the unassuming..."

He squinted at her. "Are you comparing me to a superhero?"

She rolled her eyes. "Like, duh! You're Captain Mysterious. Able to perform the Heimlich and CPR all in a single bound!"

"Oh, no." Shaking his head, he rubbed his forehead. "You have a moniker for me?"

Wishing she'd kept her mouth shut now, Kristen nodded. "Well, it wasn't me. Everyone in the bar—"

"The whole bar was talking about me?" His eyes were wide. This wasn't going the way she'd planned.

Maybe she should rethink her idea. Even if he were interested in her, she only had a few weeks before she had to return to San Diego and resume her real life.

But in the two months she'd been here she hadn't met any other guy she'd felt so drawn to. There was something about him. Something dark she recognized from her worst days in the hospital.

And she'd promised herself at her last doctor's appointment that, from that moment on, she'd live life to the fullest. And that meant sometimes taking risks.

So, maybe he'd tell her to get lost. After what she'd lived through? She could handle a little rejection.

Decided, she drew a deep breath. "You know…just a bit farther from Tradewinds is a great seafood place I've been wanting to try. But I hate going to a restaurant alone, don't you? If you like seafood, maybe we could go together sometime."

The crashing of the waves seemed louder in the long silence. Then he switched his gaze out to sea. "Uh, I'm not really good company right now."

Ouch. The fact that his answer stung a bit told her she really hadn't been prepared for rejection. Seems her glass-half-full attitude needed a reality check. "Okay." She nodded and waved a hand, took a step back, and then another, her sneakers sinking into the sand. "No worries."

She spun on her heels and jogged up to the street, yanked her bike from the rack and wheeled it across Kihei Road and into the foyer of the condominium building. Her cheeks were on fire, half embarrassed, half mad that she'd made a fool of herself. Boy, had she misread the signals.

Digging in her backpack, she pulled out her mailbox key, mumbling to herself, wanting to smack her forehead. "What an idiot. You just had to go up to a complete stranger, didn't you?" She inserted her key, yanked open the door and pulled out her mail. "Why do I do this to myself? I never learn—"

"Kristen?"

She jumped and gave a tiny shriek as she swiveled to face the voice. "Luke!" She pressed a hand to her chest and gulped. "Geez, you scared me."

"Sorry about that." He winced and reached up a hand to rub the back of his neck. Her gaze was drawn to his bicep, which was clearly familiar with a set of weights.

Then he lowered his arm and she took in the rest of him in the bright light of the lobby.

Except for his broad shoulders, he was fairly slim. Did he scuba dive? He had the perfect swimmer's body. His taut abs showed beneath his tight T-shirt and so did what looked like a set of dog tags on a long chain. Military?

"Listen, can we start over?" His voice was smooth and yet rough. Not terribly deep, but not too high either. And she picked up a trace of a Southern drawl in his accent. Possibly Texan.

It was her turn to blink at him. "Uh, sure."

A tiny smile curved the edges of his mouth. "Seafood sounds good. Tomorrow? Around seven? Meet you here?"

She smiled and nodded, feeling euphoric, as if she'd already won the *Geographic Universe* photography contest. "As it happens, I'm off tomorrow, uh, you mean later today, right? Seven's good. How about we meet at the picnic table?"

He shook his head, then stopped and nodded with a small smile. "Uh, yes, today, this evening." He stared into her eyes and his jaw shifted to the left just a fraction.

Mesmerized, Kristen could've stood there forever noting every nuance of his face, absorbing him. But he bent down and picked up her keys, offering them to her. "You dropped these."

"Oh." She hadn't even noticed. "Thank you." She took them from his outstretched palm and the same energy tingled her fingers as before. Maybe he felt it, too, because he glanced down at his hand and then back up at her, his dark eyes questioning.

"Looking forward to tomorrow, Luke." She dropped the keys into her pocket. "Good night."

He gave her a smile that was more of a grimace and waved a hand. "Good night."

She turned for the elevator, but peeked back in time to catch him checking her out. She smiled all the way to her condo.

2

LUKE CHECKED HIS WATCH again as he sat at the picnic table, elbows on knees, tapping his foot. Seven-twenty. Something told him Kristen had never been in the military. She'd have been court-martialed.

Damn it. He'd shaved for this. He'd even bought a new shirt. But it was probably a bad idea to begin with. He was only going to be here a couple more weeks.

Five minutes. Then he was out of here.

The beach was fairly crowded this time of day. He watched swimmers and snorkelers in the ocean. A dozen or so young adults clad in bikinis and cutoffs engaged in a loud game of beach volleyball. And a few families with small kids played in the surf.

All these people with normal lives. Happy lives. He remembered days like that when he was a kid. Before his dad died. He wanted normal. Happy.

Ten minutes later he stood, a hollow feeling in his

stomach, and headed down the sidewalk, not really thinking about where he was going. Just…away from here.

"Luke!"

He heard his name and glanced behind him to find Kristen racing across the street. She looked…worth waiting for. A pretty little dress that hugged her trim figure and then flared out all flirty at the bottom. High heels that made her legs look a mile long. And she'd curled her straight hair.

His cock stirred behind his zipper. Until that moment he hadn't realized how dead that part of him had been, for a long time now. He swallowed, his throat suddenly dry as she caught up to him.

"I'm so sorry I kept you waiting." Her delicate brows furrowed and she bit her bottom lip. "If I'd had your cell number, I would've called."

"It's fine." A ripe-berry scent came to him on the breeze from her shampoo and he hardened even more.

"I have a totally great reason I'm late. I'll tell you all about it at dinner."

He stared at her shoes. "You want to walk? Or, I've got a rental…"

"We can walk." But she didn't move except to turn her face to the ocean. "What a spectacular sunset."

Luke glanced across the beach and concentrated on how the sun, surrounded by vibrant peach, pink and purple altostratus clouds, was just about to sink into the sea. It didn't help his problem.

"But, then, I haven't seen one that wasn't gorgeous

since I've been here." She abruptly turned and headed north. "So, have you, uh, been out on the beach at that time of night before?"

He knew what she was fishing for. He nodded. "Once or twice."

"Ha! Well, I guess you were wondering about my behavior, huh?"

He shrugged, reluctant to admit the words *crazy* and *suicidal* had crossed his mind.

"There's just something about the moon when it's so big in the night sky. And especially here, it just seems huge, don't you think?"

Big. Huge. He closed his eyes and willed away the images those words conjured up. "I think…" He cleared his throat. "It's the lack of anything to compare its size to, when it's juxtaposed to a wide expanse of sea."

"Yes, exactly." She smiled and touched his arm. He flinched and she frowned and removed her hand. "Anyway. I was just…enjoying life." She lifted her arm and face to the sky as she had those nights.

Enjoying? Oh, to be so carefree. In his world, life was more about enduring.

"I guess that seems silly."

He glanced at her. Her voice had gone all quiet, and she was staring at her clutch purse as she picked at one of the seashell details covering it.

"No." He put his hand over hers. "That wasn't what I was thinking."

Their eyes met and held and their steps slowed. And

then she smiled, directly at him, only for him, and her blue eyes—a true sky blue—twinkled with happiness.

Luke realized two things. First, his breathing had quickened when she smiled at him. Second, he wanted to see her do it again.

She curled her hand around his and when she continued walking, she didn't let go. Palm trees and lush bougainvillea lined both sides of the road as it curved and took them farther from the edge of the ocean.

If anyone had told him a month ago he'd be strolling down the Maui coast holding hands with a gorgeous blonde, he'd have ordered them a brain scan. The scenario just didn't fit with the world he lived in. But the longer his fingers stayed entwined with hers, the stronger the sensation inside him grew. It was warmth, and a longing to slide his hand up her arm and pull her into him and hold her.

He pictured his hands circling her tiny waist, sliding up her spine, lowering his mouth to hers....

Settle down, Andrews. Think about something else.

He took stock of his surroundings. The only place he'd been since he'd flown into Maui was the beach, but he remembered the shopping center they were passing from his drive from the airport. A grocery store, a surf and dive shop, a couple of fast-food chains and even a famous coffee shop. The next block sported several bars: The Tiki Lounge, The Flaming Flamingo and the Tradewinds Bar and Grill, where Kristen worked. Where he'd gone for a cold beer.

Kristen passed that corner and turned east. About a block down was the seafood place. Once they were seated, she ordered a cola. "I serve cocktails all night," she explained, then picked up her menu. Luke ordered a beer.

"I've heard the lobster's really fresh here."

He nodded. "Sounds good."

"And some shrimp scampi?" At his nod, she repeated the order to the waiter and handed him her menu. Once he left she pulled a sheepish expression. "I really don't have a very good reason for being late except that I—I went shopping and had my hair done."

So, she'd bought this dress just for tonight? He liked that. And he didn't. His condition worsened.

She fiddled with the fork and napkin. "I didn't get back from diving until after two—"

"You've been scuba diving today?" Desperate for a distraction, he latched on to the topic.

She nodded. "I dive every day, but usually only for a few hours in the morning. I've been diving since I could walk, practically. Used to go with my dad to San Onofre State Beach every Saturday morning. We still do. In San Diego." Her expression turned wistful. "I'm living with my mom and dad at the moment. They love it, of course. But my older brother gives me a hard time about it. He's been living in L.A. since he graduated high school. He just likes to tease me, though. He's been doing that all my life. But I guess that's what older brothers are for.

"I'm only living here for a few months," she added. "You've heard of *Geographic Universe,* right?"

He nodded, but she'd already continued. "Each year they sponsor an international photography contest. I'm entering the nature category. The grand-prize winner gets their photo published in the magazine, ten thousand dollars and a chance to work with *Geographic Universe*'s head photographer."

As she talked, their food arrived. It smelled delicious and he grabbed his fork.

"But," Kristen continued, "they get tens of thousands of submissions. In order to win, my photo has to be beyond exceptional. The place where I'm diving now is a known breeding ground for the humpbacks."

Luke frowned, swallowing some shrimp. "That sounds like it could be dangerous."

She shook her head. "I don't have to get that close. Besides, they're too busy, er...mating." Her cheeks pinkened. Was she really that innocent? Or was it just first-date embarrassment?

Whoa. He was on a date. How long had it been since he'd gone on a conventional date? Before his residency. Maybe even before med school. There hadn't been time—or energy—for more than a quick roll in the sack back then. For him or the women residents. Looking back, he realized quick and impersonal had become a habit for him where his sex life was concerned.

It'd been so long since he'd thought about his life before earning his medical doctorate. Those days seemed like a lifetime ago. At eighteen he'd never given a second thought to his decision of becoming a doctor, and nothing would've stopped him. Not even the lack of a way to pay for the schooling. He'd joined the Army and never looked back.

His mom, and his sisters and brothers, had coped without him. His sisters were married with kids. Still living in Rankin, they'd visited while he'd stayed with his mom the first week of his leave. And his brothers... at least Matt was in college.

God, he felt old.

Meanwhile, Kristen appeared like a fresh-face coed. Except for her eyes. There was something in her eyes.... "How old are you?" he blurted out before thinking better of it.

Her eyes widened and her spine straightened. "Twenty-four. Why?"

What was wrong with him? He'd been so rude. "Sorry. I'm obviously not fit for polite company. You're here now to get pictures of the humpbacks and then you'll go back to San Diego?"

"Yep, whether I win or not—and it's a long-shot—I want to finish my degree. I've only got two semesters to go."

"Degree in what?"

She bit her bottom lip and closed her eyes. "Accounting." Opening her eyes, she leaned forward and poked her fork in the air. "I know. I can admit it now. I didn't even realize I was just playing it safe until..." Her brows drew together and her lips pursed. "Well, I felt like I had to give this a shot. It's a dream I didn't even dare to dream before."

Luke was mesmerized by her expressions. Everything she was feeling showed right there on her face. He couldn't imagine her ever being fraudulent, but he couldn't imagine her dealing with anything devastating either. She was too delicate, too...hopeful.

"So, I borrowed some money from my grandmother—she says she would've given it to me anyway, but I'm going to pay her interest on the loan—and decided to give myself three months to try for this contest. I dive by day and waitress by night. I've always been a photo bug and it would be a dream job to work for *Geographic Universe*. But I've only got a few more weeks left before the submission deadline and I haven't shot anything extraordinary enough."

He'd been nodding, absorbed in learning about her until her expression took on a dawning horror. "Oh, God, I've been totally talking about myself this whole time. I'm so sorry. So, tell me about you, where are you from? What do you do?" She scooped up a forkful of lobster and watched him expectantly.

Luke felt as if he'd been suddenly shoved onto center stage with a spotlight trained on him, while an audience waited breathlessly for him to perform. But how could he tell this young, carefree woman anything about what his life was like?

BEING A CITY GIRL, Kristen had never actually seen a deer caught in her headlights. But if she had, she imagined the deer would look something like Luke Andrews did right now.

Was he in the Witness Protection Program? An international spy? Maybe he had amnesia and he didn't remember where he was from or what he did for a living? That would explain the haggard look to his features and the dark circles under his eyes. She hadn't noticed those until she'd seen him in the daylight earlier. And what about his being awake at two in the morning the past few nights?

Nah. She'd watched too many soap operas in college.

She waited another half a minute—which seemed like a long time with an awkward silence hanging in the air—and then put her fork down and cleared her throat. "Luke?"

At least he met her gaze. "Sorry." Then he looked back down at his plate and took another bite.

"Is it one of those you-could-tell-me-but-then-you'd-have-to-kill-me kind of jobs?" She tried to smile and make light of it, but he was beginning to scare her. A girl could only equate mysterious with sexy up to a point.

"What?" His gaze flew back up to her and he scowled. "No. It's just...nothing you'd want to hear about."

Okay. Kristen jabbed at a shrimp.

And Luke ate.

And she ate.

Every bite or so he would look up at her. She fished around in her mind for a subject to bring up that they could discuss, but why should she? He seemed perfectly content to sit in silence.

For this she'd spent fifty-five dollars on a dress she didn't need and endured an hour with the curling iron? Maybe he regretted saying yes? Maybe he felt trapped into going out with her for politeness' sake? How depressing. That probably meant the connection she thought she'd felt between them was only in her imagination.

She jabbed at the last of her lobster, finished off her cola and came to a decision. Pulling cash from her purse, she laid enough on the table to cover the bill plus tip and scooted back in her chair. "Well, it's been, uh, interesting."

Just as she stood to go, he blurted out, "I'm a doctor in the Army medical corps, a captain."

She hesitated. "Look, you don't have to—"

"I'm here on leave." He snatched the cash off the table, held it out to her and motioned the waiter over. "And I just didn't want to ruin a nice dinner talking about it." Reaching into his back jeans pocket, he pulled out his wallet and handed the waiter a credit card.

Kristen took her cash from him and sat down. "So... you were overseas?"

"Afghanistan."

Geez. No wonder he didn't want to talk about it. It explained the things she'd seen in his eyes last night.

The waiter returned with the check and Luke signed it and stuck the card back in his wallet. Then he met her gaze, his expression serious. "I think we passed an ice cream stand on the way here."

She smiled. "I never say no to ice cream." She started to get to her feet and he jumped up and pulled her chair out. "Thank you."

His lips compressed as he gave a slow nod and indicated she should lead the way.

It had grown dark while they'd eaten dinner. Neon signs flashed from the bars, lighting the street with a multitude of colors. Foot and car traffic was heavy, but this was a tourist town and it was whale season, so Sunday nights weren't any quieter than other nights.

Kristen strolled down the street with him in silence for a while, but now the silence was comfortable. She was curious about his time served in Afghanistan, but she wouldn't pester him with questions anymore. Everyone dealt with death and dying in their own way.

She should know.

So, he was a captain in the Army. She smiled to herself, suppressed a giggle. Captain Mysterious really was a captain. And he was a doctor. That explained the Heimlich and CPR knowledge.

He stopped at the ice cream stand and bought her a dip of chocolate on a cone, but nothing for himself. As they continued down the sidewalk a dozen or more questions came to her lips, only to be stifled. He'd said he didn't want to talk about his life, and she should respect that. So she ate her ice cream and waited.

And waited. Okay, this guy took brooding to a whole new level.

"So, tell me—"

"Maybe this—"

They spoke at the same time.

"I'm sorry," he said.

"Go ahead," she said at the same time as his apology.

Kristen cringed. As far as first dates went, this one ranked right up there with the seventh-grade Sadie Hawkins dance when she'd asked John Bannister to be her date and he'd said yes and then spent the whole evening dancing with Charlene Lefavre.

Coming to a halt, Luke grimaced and rubbed the back of his neck. "I think I've been around army grunts too long."

"No, it's me. I...haven't dated much."

"That's hard to believe."

At her sudden surprise he squeezed his eyes closed and grimaced again. "I didn't mean it like— I just meant you're so pretty—"

"No worries." She put her hand on his arm. "I didn't take it the wrong way. You just caught me off guard because you've been so quiet, I thought maybe I'd cornered you into coming to dinner when you didn't really want to."

"No." He cupped her jaw in his palm and ran a thumb across her cheek. His eyes blazed into hers. And his touch heated her skin and tingled. She understood the cliché now. She really did feel as if she could fall into the deep chocolate of his eyes.

As if he suddenly realized he was caressing her cheek, he dropped his hand and stepped back.

Kristen blinked and glanced at her surroundings. The street traffic, the ocean waves crashing, the breeze riffling palm leaves all returned. When she looked back at Luke, she got the feeling he was as shocked by his action as she. Had he felt the same shivering magnetism she had? If so, his expression revealed nothing of it.

Searching for something to say, she faced forward and resumed walking. "So, did you book a tour to see the humpbacks yet?

He fell into step beside her. "Uh, no."

"Oh, you really should while you're here."

"Yeah, I'll do that."

Would he really? She remembered Amy's crazy suggestion about bringing the mystery man along on Kekoa's boat for a double date. Should she?

"You want to come out with me while I dive sometime?" Okay, that was possibly the shortest amount of time she'd ever thought something through.

"Um."

"I mean, I'd have to ask my boat driver first, and he's been acting weird lately. Don't get me wrong, he's a great guy and a really good dive partner. Very responsible. Maybe too responsible if there is such a thing. I think it stems from his heritage. He's supposedly descended from Kahekili II, the king of Maui. His father is a chieftain. I think his family is very strict about respecting their heritage and customs, and who can blame them? It's such a rich and beautiful history.

"My friend Amy—she works with me at the Tradewinds—she wants to come out on the boat with me sometime and I told her I'd ask Kekoa. I think she has a thing for him—oh, crud, I probably shouldn't have told you that. What if you come into the Tradewinds and meet her? She'd be so furious with me. Well, she'd probably forgive me if I can get Kekoa to let her on his boat. She's such a good friend, I want to help her. She's lived here a few years and she really helped me find my way around when I first got here.

"But Kekoa doesn't seem to return her attraction. Well, that's not true. He seems attracted, but he won't act on it." She frowned. "It sounds like a soap opera, doesn't it?"

They'd reached the beach across from their condos and Luke came to a stop beside the bike rack. Kristen groaned and covered her face with her hands. "I did it again. I've talked your ear off."

"I don't mind," he said softly.

She peeked between her fingers and looked up at him. One side of his mouth was curled up. Wow, an almost smile.

She glanced at the ocean. "You want to walk along the beach?"

His gaze followed hers down to the surf. "Even though there's no moon to worship tonight?"

She jerked her gaze to his face, but saw no ridicule there. Only a hint of a smile on his mouth and in his eyes.

"Guess I'll be forced to act like a normal person." With a grin, she bent to unbuckle and slip off her heels, rebuckling them around the bike rack.

He stooped to yank off his well-worn Nikes and then plopped them on the concrete beside hers. The socks followed. He'd barely set his foot down when she took his hand and tugged him down the grassy slope into the sand and all the way to the edge of the surf.

"Mmm," she moaned. "The sand feels wonderful squishing between your toes." Waves surged around her ankles. She turned to face him. He was staring at her. Hard. Piercing.

He didn't move, but she could feel something between them, pulling her to him. Something raw. As primordial as the ancient volcanoes.

The instinct was strong to step close, cup his jaw tight in her hands and kiss him. But common sense kept her immobile. She barely knew this guy. How could she be so rash? There was living life to the fullest, and then there was just plain reckless. She swallowed, frozen in indecision.

And the moment passed. He dropped her hand and glanced away, across the dark ocean and then over his shoulder down the coast, and stuck his hands in his pockets. He took one step away, splashing through the waves.

Drawing in a deep breath, she followed, glancing up at the millions of stars so clear in the sky. They seemed so close, she felt as if she could just reach up and grab one. She felt again that joy of just being alive. How very lucky she was to be on the earth to taste and smell and see and touch all the beautiful things around her.

After she'd walked beside him for a hundred yards or so in the surf, foam tickling her ankles, she couldn't help but wonder what was going through his mind. "You're lucky to have a condo with a balcony facing the ocean," she said.

"It's not my condo. It belongs to a buddy of mine."

"Wow. Everyone should have buddies like that."

He shrugged. "He thinks I…"

When he didn't continue, she glanced over and studied him. His jaw hitched to the left just a fraction. He'd done that last night when he seemed to be wrestling with himself over something.

"I haven't been sleeping very well lately."

That did explain his presence on the beach at 2:00 a.m. Why did she suspect that was an understatement? "Has staying on a picturesque tropical island helped?"

He grimaced. "Not so far."

Her mind was churning with ideas. "How long do you have before you go back?"

"Three weeks."

"What all have you tried?"

He frowned. "What do you mean?"

She clasped his arm and came to a halt. "I assume you've already talked to a psychotherapist, but, what about massage therapy? Aromatherapy? Hypnosis? Um... What else... Oh! Yoga!"

He got that deer in the headlights look again. "I—I work out."

"Or what about hiking? Have you been to see the Alelele Falls? They're my favor—" She noticed his hardened expression. "What's the matter?"

"I'm not some head case you have to fix."

"Oh, no, I didn't mean—"

His eyes narrowed. "Did John put you up to this?"

"John?"

He stared at her a moment longer and then turned away. "Never mind," he said over his shoulder and headed back in the direction they'd come from. "Guess I can add paranoid to my list of symptoms," he muttered under his breath.

What had she done? Her stomach sank like her diving weight belt. Kristen jogged to catch up to him. "Luke." She caught his arm again. "I'm so sorry I butted in. I tend to get overenthusiastic sometimes. It's a bad habit of mine."

He let her stop him and turned to face her, his eyes closed, his expression pained. "No." He took her hand and squeezed it. "I should be the one apologizing. I was right the first time. I'm just not good company right now. Forgive me, Kristen. It's not you, okay?"

"Hey, I know things started out kind of rocky, but—"

"Have a great time the rest of your stay here, and good luck winning that contest."

"Luke, please."

"I'll walk you back to our building." He put his hand at the small of her back and gestured for her to accompany him.

Reluctantly, Kristen headed toward the condo. She tightened her lips, determined not to utter one more word to the stupid man.

No. He wasn't stupid. It was her fault. She'd jumped in as usual and blabbered on without thinking. It was just something about coming so close to death that made her not want to waste time on small talk and second-guessing herself. She'd tried, but...

Now she'd ruined it with him. The best she could hope for was that it wouldn't be awkward to run into him around the condominium. But it's not as if they'd had any real future together. A hot vacation fling for a few weeks had been the most it ever could've been. And even that was a glass-half-full assumption.

Oh, but what a fling it might have been.

3

THE SOLDIER LOOKED UP at Luke with big, dark eyes full of confidence. Confidence Luke didn't deserve.

"You can fix me, can't ya, Doc?" The private couldn't have been twenty. His young body was shivering, bloodied, full of shrapnel. But Luke probably could've dealt with that. It was the gaping hole in the kid's chest cavity Luke couldn't repair.

The trauma room was a cacophony of dreadful sounds. Agonized screams, mortar rounds blasting outside and doctors and nurses yelling orders and information.

He avoided the soldier's gaze and ordered a morphine drip to manage the worst of the kid's pain. That's all he could do. There were dozens more he could help. Ones who had a chance. He started to leave but the private grabbed his wrist and Luke forced himself to meet the soldier's eyes.

"My pocket," he said in a strangled voice. "Make sure the letter gets to my mom, okay?"

Luke set his jaw, emotion tightening his throat, threatening to overcome him. Swallowing back his howling grief, he reached into the private's blood-soaked shirt pocket, pulled out a dripping folded piece of notepaper and slid it into the pants pocket of his scrubs. Then he looked back at the private to reassure him. But the boy was gone.

Luke gently closed the kid's eyes.

Then the lights flickered and Luke felt hands clutching at him and bodies crushing him in. They tugged at him, pulling him in all directions. An Afghani National, a little Afghan boy, a burned woman and dozens of American soldiers, all dead, all blaming him.

LUKE AWOKE ON A STRANGLED cry. Breathing hard, he rolled off the bed, paced to the living room and stood at the balcony doors until the last vestiges of the dream faded.

He couldn't stop shivering, so he trudged to the bathroom, splashed water on his face. He wasn't getting better. He stared at his shaking hands and willed them to still. The tremors seemed to worsen. How could he suture a patient with these hands? My God. What if he couldn't? How could he return to his unit if he couldn't get himself under control? He'd be a disgrace to his colleagues, his superiors. "Coward."

Spinning on his heel he punched the wall. The dog jumped and whimpered. *Terrific.* He'd dented the

Sheetrock in John's condo. Wow, he really was losing it. He'd be sure to remember to fix that wall before he left.

He hadn't been out of the condo the past couple of days except to let the dog out into the back courtyard. Maybe he'd better get out of here before he did any more damage. He checked the clock. One forty-five. He could go down and be back before Kristen got home. After their first meeting, he'd bought a collar and leash for the mutt.

Running into her shouldn't matter.

But it did.

He found himself on the beach, thankfully deserted this time of night, striding down the coast. Details of the nightmare came back to him, as real as if that private had died tonight. Why did these deaths haunt him? Even if Luke wasn't serving in Afghanistan, fatalities were always a risk for a surgeon. What the hell was wrong with him?

A few more days of this and he'd have to resort to trying a sleep aid. He remembered Kristen's suggestions. Massage therapy? Hypnosis? Would any of that really work?

Kristen.

He missed her.

Which was ridiculous. He barely knew her.

He slowed and came to a stop. He'd always been quiet. His mother used to say he thought too much. Left alone with his thoughts, especially lately, he could get morose. Kristen might've been embarrassed about hogging the conversation, but he'd liked it. She didn't constantly ask him what he was thinking. And he hadn't felt as if he had to make polite small talk with her. When he'd been around her, he hadn't thought about death so much. Her smile and her chatter had kept him entranced, and her positive outlook had been contagious.

Without giving himself time to rethink it, he toed off his sneakers and stepped into the water, letting the waves splash around his ankles and calves, digging his toes into the wet sand. He kicked at the water and let the spray blow into his face. The dog thought this was a great game and barked and splashed around in the waves.

As a remedy for dark moods, this was working fairly well. Maybe there was something to Kristen's advice. He closed his eyes and thought of her blond hair blowing in the breeze, of her blue eyes full of life and laughter smiling up at him. Why had he blown her off the other night? He couldn't come up with one good reason now. Except that he was a colossal moron.

Striding out of the water, he grabbed up his sneakers and headed to the picnic table. He sat, leaned his elbows on the table behind him and dropped his head back to look at the stars. The dog decided to shake the water off his coat right next to Luke, spraying him with salty, hairy water. Now he needed to wait to be dry before going in.

His excuse paid off when he saw Kristen riding her bike down Kihei Road as usual. When she veered toward the condo he realized he'd expected her to leave her bike at the rack and head down to the beach. But she hadn't.

He jumped up and jogged across the street after her. "Kristen," he called out as he caught up to her.

She glanced behind her, swerved, and her front wheel hit the curb. The bike pitched forward and she screamed and flew off, headfirst.

Reflexes took over. Luke leaped to try to catch her just as she landed onto the grass. Her helmet knocked him on the chin and he lay there stunned, catching his breath. One of her elbows poked into his ribs. Then she shifted and her elbow was replaced with soft, cushiony breasts. His body reacted and he bit back a groan.

His arms were around her and he could feel her bra strap under her T-shirt beneath one palm and a smooth thigh beneath the other. If he slid his hand up a couple inches higher his fingers could caress the soft flesh under the hem of her shorts. He closed his eyes and willed his erection to go away.

How sick was that when she could be hurt? "Are you all right?" He began a rudimentary examination of the bones in her arms and wrists. Nothing felt broken.

"Luke?" She raised her head, unsnapped her helmet and pulled it off. Her hair fell across his face until she turned her head to face him. As he drew a breath, the fragrance of wild berries invaded his senses, attached itself to his bloodstream and shot straight to his groin. Her shampoo.

She looked stunned. "What are you doing here?" Her voice quivered and he snapped back to reality.

"Does anything hurt?"

"I'm fine." She lifted off him and he had to quell the urge to not let her go.

As she sat up, so did he, taking note of how she favored her left shoulder. "You *are* hurt." He gently explored her clavicle and she winced.

"It doesn't feel broken. On a scale of one to ten, how bad is the pain?"

She chuckled. "I'm fine, Doc. Just bruised." She gingerly got to her feet and Luke hurriedly stood and tried to help her, his arm curving around her waist.

"Careful. You could have other injuries."

"Nah. You broke my fall." She started brushing off grass and dirt, and, reluctantly, he dropped his arm. "What about you? Are you hurt?"

He could feel a few sore areas that would probably bruise, but otherwise he was fine. "If I hadn't scared you, you wouldn't have fallen." He bent to haul up her bike and inspect the damage. The front wheel was mangled. "Looks like I owe you a new bicycle."

"Oh, no!" She stared at her crooked front wheel. "Well, maybe it can be fixed. Anyway, I bought it secondhand." She looked up from the wheel rim to meet his gaze. "So…were you out here waiting for me?"

Her light blue eyes seemed to pierce straight into

the deepest part of him. What did she see? "I guess I was." He swallowed, feeling like a first-class jerk. "I don't suppose you'd give me a second chance and have dinner with me tomorrow night?"

Her brows rose. "I work tomorrow night."

"Oh, right." He nodded. "Of course. I understand." He waved a hand. "Let me help you get this inside." He picked up the bike by its frame and headed for the condo's lobby.

"Luke," she called, not moving.

"Yeah?" He stopped and half turned.

Her teeth flashed in a quick grin. "Come with me on the boat in the morning."

"IN THE MORNING" actually meant about four hours later. But Luke wasn't complaining. He wouldn't have slept anyway. She'd asked for his cell number and given him hers just in case he changed his mind.

But he wouldn't have.

As they approached a large fishing boat, Kristen cupped her hands around her mouth and yelled, "Permission to come aboard?"

A tall, native Hawaiian stepped out of the cabin, smiled at Kristen and waved them on board. *Ho'opono* was painted on the hull in bold black letters. Kristen told Luke it was Hawaiian for *Faithful*. Once they'd boarded, Kristen introduced Kekoa to Luke as her dive partner and boat driver.

Kekoa shook his hand. Firmly. And there was a glint in his eye, as if he were sizing Luke up. Was the guy trying to establish a prior claim? Then he noticed a red-head with long legs sitting on a cushioned seat in the stern of the boat. Kristen introduced her as her friend and coworker, Amy Burrows. Luke vaguely recalled Kristen talking about her friend the other night. But not the particulars. Amy got lazily to her feet to shake his hand with a conspiratorial grin, picked up a basket of muffins then disappeared behind Kekoa into the cabin.

Kristen cast off the stern- and bowlines and within minutes they were in open sea.

Luke tugged his U.S. Army ball cap down tighter against the wind. He hadn't been out on the ocean since he was a kid and his family had rented a beach house one summer in Galveston. That had been a lifetime ago.

But the salty sea spray hitting his face and the boat slamming down against the choppy waves started a video playing in his head of that carefree time in his life. When his father had still been alive. The kind of joyful existence he'd like to attain in his life now, but seemed so far beyond his reach he wouldn't know how to start.

"Have you ever seen such crystal clear water?" Kristen appeared beside him against the railing at the rear of the boat, staring out across the ocean. She was using her hand to shade her face, but her eyes and nose were still adorably scrunched against the sun. Without makeup this morning she looked so fresh, so natural, he wanted to soak in her wholesomeness and save it for the lonely dark of night.

Luke shook his head. "Where are we headed?" He had to shout over the roar of the motor.

"Molokini Crater." She caught a lock of hair that had escaped her ponytail blowing across her face and tucked it behind her ear. She motioned for him to follow her and headed around the cabin to the front of the boat. Then she squinted one eye and pointed. "You can just see the crescent-shaped formation ahead."

Luke was more interested in staring at her in a short, black wet suit that hugged her body and showed every womanly curve. An image flashed in his mind of his hands caressing his way down and around those curves.

She turned back to face him and he jerked his gaze out to the rock she'd pointed at. "Um, so, that's where the humpbacks are?"

"Sometimes. But Molokini is mostly famous for snorkeling. I told Kekoa we'd go there since you and Amy are with us today. It's a partially submerged volcanic crater, and inside the rim you can see the most gorgeous fish and coral, mantas, eels, even a few spinner dolphins. Kekoa has extra snorkeling equipment on board if you want to go in."

"I'd like that."

"Afterward, I'm going to dive the Backside. About eighty feet down are some rare species of fish, plus white-tipped sharks. The water is so clear—"

"Hold on a minute." Luke had to interrupt her there. "Did you just say sharks?" Hairs on the back of his neck stood up.

"Oh, the shark caves are down about a hundred and twenty feet. It's the current I have to worry about."

And this was supposed to make him feel better? "Have you dived here before?"

"Of course. Well, not the Backside, but I'll be fine. Kekoa dives with me and he's very safety conscious, believe me. Oh, we're almost there. Good. There's only one other boat here so far. I better go tell him where I want to tie the moorings. We don't drop anchor because of the coral."

As Kristen disappeared into the cabin, Amy came out and approached him. "Hey, I brought muffins, if you're hungry. Blueberry, banana and cinnamon."

"Thanks. I'm good for now."

She leaned her forearms on the railing, but turned her head to look at him. "I'm so glad you came today, too."

"Why is that?" Luke couldn't help but notice the red-head wore makeup and had a pair of expensive-looking sunglasses on top of her head holding her long hair off her face. But it still blew wildly in the wind.

"Kekoa is diving with Kris, and I don't want to sit up here all alone." She pouted pretty red lips.

Aah. He nodded.

She wore a pair of white short shorts and a red halter that bared her midriff and a good portion of her cleavage. Plus a very impractical pair of wedged high heels. The motor sputtered off and the boat drifted to a stop in the bay. With her height and the way she was bent over leaning on the railing, Luke would've had to be blind or gay not to notice her ample breasts. But he got the feeling she wasn't trying to be overtly sexy, it just seemed to be her style.

"Do you come out here often with them?"

Amy shook her head. "Never been. I've been begging Kris to take me for weeks. Do you dive?"

"No. I've never had the time. You?"

She shuddered. "I think I'd get claustrophobic with that mask over my nose and that breathing thingy in my mouth."

"So, no snorkeling either?"

She shook her head.

"Then I guess we're stuck watching the boat."

"Oh, don't let me keep you from snorkeling," Amy said.

"Kekoa can keep Amy company while you and I go." Kristen appeared behind Luke and he shifted to face her. "In fact, I don't even have to dive today. I could just snorkel with you."

The concern in her eyes, so blue they put these tropical waters to shame, baffled him. Would she actually forgo her diving just for him? "Don't you have a contest to win?"

"Well…yeah."

After his father died, Luke had been determined to become a doctor. There was no money for college, much less medical school. Still, he'd found a way to make it happen. And he proudly served his country for the education the Army had given him.

He stepped close and gripped her shoulders in his hands. "Don't let anyone keep you from your goal."

She tilted her head and blinked. The next thing he knew, her hands were cupping his face and her mouth touched his and was gone again. When he opened his eyes she was smiling up at him. "Thank you."

His lips tingled. His body hardened. He wanted to pull her against him and show her what a real kiss could be like between them. Before he could put the thought into action Kekoa called to her and she swiveled away and grabbed her diving equipment.

Kristen felt the pressure of the water closing in on her as she neared eighty feet. She'd descended slowly to acclimate, using a line from the boat, and had been snapping photos of the vivid coral and anemone growing on the reef for about—she checked her oxygen level—ten minutes while she made her way to this depth.

Schools of brightly colored fish darted everywhere and a ray swam lazily by. Kristen let go of the rope and moved closer to the reef. As she swam around the curve in the formation to the Backside, the current got stronger. She took her reef hook, secured herself to the reef and then let the current take her a bit farther along the crater, captivated by the natural shelves formed in the rock.

Her camera at the ready, she snapped photos of red sponge, orange tube coral and a few iridescent jellyfish.

She gasped. A crown-of-thorns starfish! So rare. This might be her winning photo. If she could get just the perfect angle and lighting. She looked back at Kekoa and signaled her intent to move farther around. He nodded and followed.

Holding on to an outcropping of rock, she tugged her reef hook out so she could get closer to the starfish, carefully moved to her right and reattached her hook. But as she drifted toward the starfish, the reef crumbled beneath her hook and before she could blink, the powerful current swept her away.

After allowing one curse word in her head, she tried to stay calm. Panicking wouldn't help.

Instead, she swam for her life, fighting the current for every foot back to where Kekoa waited. But she wasn't even maintaining her position. Kekoa was getting farther and farther away and the panic she was trying to hold at bay was rising in her chest.

Keep swimming. It will be okay.

Kekoa was pulling his cave line from his retractor. Making a loop at the end, he sent it into the current. She'd probably only have one shot to grab it. If she missed, she'd be carried away trying for it, and the line was only five-hundred feet.

As it shot toward her she reached out and snatched it, then tightened the loop around one arm. After allowing for a moment to rest and her breathing to calm, she pulled herself along the taut rope. Kekoa held on to the rough rock with both hands, not willing to risk it crumbling from his hook, also. The retractor tugged at his belt.

Finally she made it to him and they swam for safer water. Her heart raced at the close call. She signaled Kekoa her thanks and he gestured that he wanted to surface. She nodded. Her ragged breathing was using up all her oxygen, anyway.

Waiting those two minutes to equalize before surfacing had never seemed to take so long. As she yanked off her fins, mask and regulator, she grabbed the lower rungs of the *Ho`opono*'s ladder. Her muscles felt like jelly and she couldn't catch a breath. Now that the crisis had passed, she started shaking uncontrollably. She couldn't make her muscles pull her up the ladder.

"Luke?" Geez, was that her voice all wobbly?

His head appeared over the side of the boat. "Kristen? What's the matter? Are you all right?"

She tried to rein in her terror as he extended his hand to help her up the ladder.

The last few rungs, he grasped her under the arms and hauled her up onto the deck. Even with all her heavy equipment he lifted her as if she weighed nothing.

Embarrassingly, her knees buckled when she tried to stand and she fell into his arms. He took her regulator from her shaking hand, pulled off her mask and wrapped his arms around her. She laid her cheek against his hard, warm chest. His biceps strained beneath her hands. She felt home, secure, cared for.

A girl could get used to that.

She drew in a deep breath, then let out a long sigh and tried to stop shivering. But she tightened her hold.

"Are you all right?" He moved his hands beneath her arms and pushed her away to study her face. His thumbs rubbed along the sides of her breasts. Another sensation entirely now robbed her of speech. How could any woman think straight while he did that?

She managed to nod and then slid her arms around his waist and laid her cheek against his chest once more. She just wanted to stay in his arms and hold him and be held.

"Oh, Kekoa, look at your hands!" Amy cried out.

Kristen turned her head to see Amy tending Kekoa's bleeding palms. Guilt ripped her up inside.

"What the hell happened down there?" Luke asked, guiding Kristen to a seat and lowering her onto it. He took one of Kekoa's hands and scrutinized it. "Tell Amy where to find the first-aid kit," he ordered Kekoa and then took his other hand to examine it. "This cut should probably have a couple of stitches."

"No stitches," Kekoa replied quickly, after describing the wall where the first-aid box hung. "Just patch me up, Doc."

Luke stilled and stared at the wounds as if he saw something else, then he blinked and seemed to come back. What was that about?

She unzipped her BCD and slipped it off her shoulders. While Luke treated Kekoa's hands, with Amy assisting like a veteran RN, Kristen unclipped her belt and then went to inspect the damage to her partner's hands.

"Kekoa, I am so sorry." She gently touched a finger to the gauze wrapped around his palm.

"I'm fine."

"So, what happened?" Luke asked again.

"My reef hook didn't hold." Kristen plopped into a seat, exhausted. "The current swept me away, but Kekoa's quick thinking saved the day." She smiled at her dive partner.

Kekoa held her gaze unsmiling. "You would have done the same for me."

"It sounds positively horrifying," Amy said. "I don't know how you can talk about it so casually, Kris."

Kristen didn't want to think about it anymore. She'd faced death before and one thing she was good at: taking life one day, one hour, even one minute at a time. "I'm starving. Let's head back and get some lunch."

"Oh, that sounds good." Amy packed up the first-aid kit and followed Kekoa as he moved toward the cabin. "I know just the place. It's a little bistro by the marina. Do you like the food there, Kekoa?"

"Yes, but I can't join you," he answered. "I have other business."

"Oh, no." She pouted. "Well, that blows."

Kekoa turned back with a raised eyebrow. "Blows?"

"Er…I mean, I'm disappointed." Amy bit her lip.

Without another word, Kekoa turned, entered the cabin and started the engine.

Poor Amy. Kristen had tried to warn her. Kekoa was such a traditional guy. His father was a chief. His *Ohana* was practically considered royalty, and they were all about honor, ancestors and bloodlines. It was bad enough he wanted to start a tourist business. They would never approve of him dating someone they hadn't vetted as a proper wife. They especially would not approve of a cocktail waitress.

Kristen was at a loss as to what to say to Amy, although she could usually be distracted if Kristen mentioned shopping. "Hey, isn't that bistro right next to the little shop with all the cute earrings?" Kristen asked her.

"I guess so." Amy stared after Kekoa. "I think I'll go home, though. I don't know how you get up so early every morning and work so late at night."

Kristen sometimes wondered herself, but she didn't say anything. She knew Amy wasn't really tired. If only she could help her friend somehow. But talking to Kekoa would make things worse. She stood and put her arm around her friend. "I'm sorry, Amy."

Amy pasted on a bright smile. "No worries." She flounced off around the cabin to the front of the boat and stood at the railing with her chin up and her hair blowing behind her as though she was queen of the world. Kristen knew that was an act. She almost followed her, but then thought it best to leave her alone for the moment. Let her deal with her feelings in private.

Kristen turned to Luke. He'd been quiet throughout the exchange. He sat with his elbows on his knees as the boat changed direction and headed for shore. His face held no expression. What was he thinking?

Maybe he thought she was an incompetent diver. That she had caused her dive partner to get hurt. Maybe he wished he hadn't come today and gotten mixed up in all this? Depression seeped into her chest. It seemed as if the whole outing had become a disaster.

And she realized now, only when it seemed it was not to be, how much she'd wanted something to happen between herself and Luke.

She wanted to make love with him.

Which was huge for her. Because she hadn't been intimate with anyone since she'd lost her right breast.

4

KEKOA PULLED BACK ON the throttle, killed the engine and let the *Ho`opono* drift into dock. He checked behind him, but Kristen had already disembarked, grabbed the stern line and secured it to the moorings. Her man, Luke, jumped off and secured the towline.

Despite the accident today, Kristen was a good partner, a sensible woman.

Unlike the redhead who appeared in his line of vision, taking Luke's hand to help her step off the boat in those ridiculous shoes. She didn't even dress sensibly. Everything about her irritated Kekoa. Including the erotic daydreams he couldn't seem to prevent. He pictured himself untying her halter and cupping her full breasts, rubbing his thumbs over her stiff nipples.

No. It was shameful to have such thoughts about her when he was practically engaged to another woman. The marriage between himself and Mahina had been arranged when they were both children. He didn't want to marry Mahina, and he was pretty sure she loved another. But they were both bound by honor to unite their families.

And if he weren't?

He closed his eyes and remembered Amy's tender ministrations to his hands earlier. Her perfume was like her: exotic and sensual. Even now it lingered in the air here in his cabin. If he were a different man, he'd have her in his bed before the sun set tonight. But it was just as well. If she were his woman, he would never allow her to work in that bar and flirt with other men all night.

"Hey, I forgot my basket."

He spun on his heel to find the object of his thoughts standing just inside the door to his cabin. He looked out at the dock as Kristen and Luke drove away in a Jeep.

Amy took a step and grabbed her basket off the console. "Kris said to tell you goodbye," Amy continued. "She tried to get your attention, but you must have been busy with boat stuff."

Boat stuff? He remembered the first time he met Amy. He'd dropped in to the Tradewinds one evening to give Kristen the new brochures he'd had printed up. Amy had brought him a drink and hung around to talk.

At first, he'd admit, he'd been so attracted to her he'd wanted nothing more than to invite her back to his place. But the longer they talked, the more he could see they had nothing in common. She loved beach volleyball and shopping, the latest celebrity gossip.

How could he be attracted to someone like that?

"Well. Thanks for letting me come along today."

He nodded. "*Mahalo*. For the muffins. They were very good."

She gave him a small smile and then turned to duck out of the cabin.

"Amy." He caught her arm and pulled her back. Perhaps he yanked too hard. She bumped into his chest. Her dainty upturned nose was mere millimeters away from his. She had a sprinkling of freckles across the bridge. *Hupo!* Fool. He'd just hardened. Over freckles.

Her eyes were wide and staring into his. Without thinking it through, he kissed a freckle, and let his lips linger. She gasped and her chest moved against his. He groaned. A man could only resist so much. He took her mouth with his and moved it over hers with a desperation he'd never allowed himself before. He sucked her tongue into his mouth and played with it, then slipped his tongue into her mouth.

Her arms slid around his neck and her hips pushed against his. Her stomach rubbed his cock until he thought he might burst. Before he realized it she had his shirt unbuttoned and was kissing her way down his throat. He tried to untie her halter, but gave up. Too slow. He grabbed the bottom, lifted it above her breasts and bent to lick one rigid nipple.

Her delighted cry spurred him to pull it between his teeth. He palmed her other breast and squeezed the nipple between his thumb and finger. "Amy," he rasped as he moved to draw on her other nipple. *"Nou No Ka `I`ini."* I desire you.

He unzipped her shorts, yanked them and her panties down and then lifted her onto his console. Just as he'd imagined her. Whimpering, she grasped the back of his head and hooked a leg around his hip. While he scrambled to pull down his swimsuit, she produced a condom out of what seemed to be thin air and expertly rolled it on him.

He gripped her hips and pushed into her hard and fast, and she gasped and closed her eyes. She was tight and hot, and the sensation nearly brought him to his knees. He wanted to savor the feeling of her surrounding him.

She opened her eyes and their gazes met. And for a split second he thought he saw fear or uncertainty cross her features. Then she was kissing him, and his body begged him to move. He pulled out and pushed back in and she made a little sound at the back of her throat. Soon she was moaning against his lips to the rhythm of his thrusts.

This was no slow seduction, but raw need surging through his veins. She reached between them and fingered her clit. As she dropped her head back and cried out, it sent him over the edge. He buried his nose in her spicy-smelling neck and erupted like burning lava from an active volcano.

Gasping for breath, he tightened his arms around her, needing an anchor to the earth.

It could've been minutes or hours that passed until he slowly regained his senses. Whatever had possessed him gradually left his body and he became aware of his surroundings. They were in his cabin. Both of them half-naked in full view of anyone on the pier who might happen by. And she was running her fingers through his hair and he was holding her tightly against him, still inside her.

What had he just done?

He dropped his arms from around her and stepped back. Checking the dock to see if anyone was watching, he turned his back to Amy and he pulled himself together.

Movement behind him told him she was doing the same.

Every curse word he knew flew through his brain. How could he have lost control? He'd not been raised to disrespect women this way. Drawing a deep breath, he turned to face her, his mouth already open to apologize.

But she reached up and covered his mouth with her hand. "Don't."

He took her wrist and removed her hand. "Don't what?"

A small, knowing smile curved her lips. "Don't ruin my day with whatever you were going to say." She pulled her sunglasses down from the top of her head onto her nose, grabbed her basket and left his cabin without looking back.

As he watched, she stepped off his boat without a helping hand from anyone, sauntered down the dock and got into a rusted-out Toyota.

Kekoa rubbed his stomach. What had he done? And what was he going to do about it now?

"Now you've been officially lei'd." Kristen dropped the silk plumeria lei over Luke's head and grinned up at him.

He probably looked like an idiot, but he didn't care. He shook his head and tried to look bored, but inside he was smiling. "I'm not buying this." He took it off and placed it back on the rack with the hundreds of others in the tacky souvenir shop off Kihei Road. Kristen had insisted they stroll along visiting all the tourist traps... er...shops after lunch at the marina.

"Oh, you're no fun." She wrinkled her nose at him, shoved his shoulder and then moved on to the next shelf of items.

No fun? She had no idea. It'd taken everything inside him earlier to recover from the damned flashback on the boat. He'd never experienced a flashback before, but he didn't know what else to call what had happened to him. One minute he was looking at Kekoa's hands, the next he was back at the hospital in Kabul and that private with his legs blown off was looking up at him saying, "Just patch me up, Doc."

Now he was having nightmares while he was wide-awake? What was he going to do?

"Luke?"

He snapped back to the souvenir shop with its grass hula skirts and coconut-shell bras and…the most beautiful girl he'd ever met. She might not be conventionally gorgeous, but there was just something about her. Something bright and warm and captivating.

To have her smile at him like she was, he'd dutifully look at shark-tooth necklaces, wiggling dashboard hula girls and child-size Hawaiian warrior helmets made with feathers similar to a kid's Indian headdress.

"Oh, look!" She gasped. "Pineapple hard candy and powdered poi. I have to get these." She grabbed up a bag and a small white jar and took them to the checkout. Luke followed, wondering what the heck powdered poi was, but confident that Kristen would tell him.

"Have you ever had poi, Luke? Don't let the purple color fool you, it's delicious."

Inside the glass display case next to the register were finer pieces of jewelry. Luke scoped out the earrings and then studied Kristen's ear for a piercing hole. She wasn't wearing any jewelry, but her ears were pierced. He made an impulsive decision.

"Thank you," Kristen told the shop owner as she returned her wallet to her purse and stepped outside.

"There's an outdoor café," Luke said. "How about something to drink?"

"Okay." Kristen smiled at him and, like it did every time, it hit him in the gut. As soon as they were seated and had ordered, he excused himself. But instead of heading for the restroom, he doubled back and ducked into the shop.

He had no idea what she might like, but something bright seemed safe. He made his purchase and slipped back to their table with it tucked safely in his pocket.

He couldn't wait to see her face when he gave them to her. But then, he felt as though he could stare at her for hours or days, and never grow tired of her expressions, or her chatter.

"Luke?"

He blinked, and stared at her. "I'm sorry. What were you saying?" He focused on her blue eyes, which were slightly confused.

"I just wondered where you went just now."

So, she'd noticed him going back to the shop? "Where I went?" He cleared his throat. "I, uh…" Should he just come clean? "What do you mean?"

"Oh, nothing. It's probably just me. But you seemed to be somewhere else mentally there for a minute."

"Oh." Relief mixed with embarrassment. She must think he was the slowest jerk on the island. "Yeah. No, sorry about that."

She tilted her head and looked so confused. "Let's start over, okay?" She opened her bag of candy and popped one in her mouth. "Want one?"

"No, thanks." He just wanted to watch her as she sucked and moved it around her mouth. He was mesmerized.

"Luke?"

"Yes?" His voice was all scratchy. He grabbed his bottle of water and took a long swallow.

"I'm glad you still wanted to get some lunch after the way things ended on the boat."

"I was only worried you might not be up to it after the scare you had." This morning he'd had to amend his original impression of her as delicate. Anyone who would dive down eighty feet in shark-infested waters, almost get swept away in a deadly current then be worried about some guy she barely knew, well, as his mother used to say, she had more brass than a marching band.

"And I was afraid you'd think I was an incompetent diver."

He covered her hand with his own. "No way. Just the opposite."

She dropped her gaze to their joined hands, slowly turned hers and rubbed her thumb along the top of his. White-hot need blazed through him. He could see the hunger she wasn't even trying to hide in her eyes. He inhaled his surprise. Her thumb still caressed the back of his hand, burning a path along his skin. He wanted to feel her touching him everywhere. If he closed his eyes, he could imagine what it felt like to have her fingers trail up his arm to his shoulder. Her hands would explore his chest until he pulled her into his arms and their bodies collided, skin to skin.

What would she look like without clothes on? Her

wet suit, and even her shorts and T-shirts, left much to the imagination. But she'd be tanned from surfing in a bikini. Her hips were slim, her stomach flat. Her breasts were small, but shapely.

"Luke?"

He blinked and was back at the café with her sitting beside him, her clothes very much on, and felt his face heat. One touch of her hand and his mind went straight to picturing her naked.

Her free hand lifted, cupped his jaw and turned his head to face her. Desire was still there in her eyes. He leaned in, angled his head and gave her the barest hint of a kiss, a test, a query. When he pulled away, she followed, pressing her lips to his with a sense of urgency that answered his question.

Yes.

With a tiny moan she sat back. "I was thinking…" She was staring at his mouth.

"Yes?" Her fingers were so delicate compared to his. He took her hand and kissed her knuckles, then kissed her palm, his lips nibbling to her wrist.

She made a little sound in her throat. Her eyes were half-closed, unfocused. "I, uh…"

Her wrist and arm were so slender, he kissed his way up.

"Luke, can we go?"

"Okay." He stood, pulled her chair out for her, and they both practically ran to his Jeep. While he drove, she casually put her hand on his thigh. He glanced over at her and she was watching the road ahead with a perfectly innocent expression.

Except a secret smile played over her features and she slowly caressed her way up to an inch or so from his crotch and then down to his knee. Then back up again. He was instantly and painfully erect. Her touch was the most erotic thing he'd ever experienced.

In record time he was pulling into a space in the parking garage, unsnapping his seat belt and going around, taking her hand as she jumped out of the Jeep. The elevator took forever and then they were at her door and she was fumbling with her keys.

He almost took them from her, but he doubted he'd be any faster at unlocking the door. He could barely see straight and his breathing was shallow. The curse word she mumbled might have been the cutest thing he'd ever heard. While she tried the key one more time, he focused on the smooth skin of her nape, left so vulnerable by her ponytail. Setting his hands at her waist, he lowered his head to softly place his lips on her right carotid artery. "Your pulse is elevated."

She angled her head to give him greater access. "It is?"

"Mmm-hmm." He took full advantage, letting his mouth follow the artery down to her shoulder and linger. "You might want to see a doctor about that."

"Oh?" At this point she'd given up trying to unlock her door. "Can you recommend a good one?" The last word drifted into a quiet moan.

"As it happens, I can." He turned her in his arms, and at last—at last he took her mouth. Her hands slid up his shoulders and she opened to him. Hesitant at first, he kept the kiss light, lingering on the edge of a fierce desire.

It was Kristen who deepened the kiss, digging her short nails into his scalp. His control almost gone, Luke tightened his arms around her and explored her mouth with abandon. She met his tongue with her own and sent a shock of lust straight to the blood already throbbing between his legs. He groaned and broke the kiss, took the keys and within seconds had the door open.

Without releasing him, Kristen stepped through and he'd barely followed when she raised her lips to his once more. The kiss was deep, sensual. Profound. She tasted of pineapple and he knew he'd never again taste that fruit without thinking of her.

He slid his hands around her waist and set about enjoying the feel of her lips moving in and out and over and under his. Playfully, her tongue darted out and touched his. He might have moaned, or maybe it was her, but the sound made him aware he'd left the door open, so he kicked it shut.

She chuckled, her mouth still beneath his, and he could feel her smile. He smiled with her, reveling in this amazing thing that was happening to him. It was more than just the anticipation of sex, although that was a pulsing need, too. It was a lifting of a burden deep inside just knowing she wanted him, this sexy, fun-loving woman. This wasn't some quick exhausted relieving of tension with someone between long, tiring hospital shifts.

"Kristen." He scooped her up, surprising a short cry from her. He took her to the sofa, laid her down on the cushions and followed her, his chest against hers, his hips pushing into hers. He stared at her beautiful smile and then lowered his head and molded his mouth to hers, taking and giving, deepening and deepening even more.

Her hands ran through his hair, down his back, and the tips of her fingers burrowed under the waistband of his jeans at the small of his back. Need ramped up and threatened his control. He slid his arm out from beneath her, lifted her T-shirt. Still deep in her kiss, he cupped her satin-covered breast.

She jerked her mouth from his and knocked his hand away. He stilled above her, catching his breath, confused, wary, his hand still in midair.

She'd squeezed her eyes closed and her arms were folded against her chest.

He pushed off her and sat on the other end of the sofa. "I'm sorry, did I—"

"No, it was nothing you did." She hadn't moved or opened her eyes.

"Kristen?" He leaned over to brush her hair off her cheek and she flinched.

"You know I totally forgot I have to work tonight."

Luke hesitated, confused as hell. What had he done? He thought she might at least open her eyes and look at him and smile. This was Kristen, after all. Joyful, blow kisses to the moon and dance in the ocean Kristen. "All right." He got to his feet, stuffed his fingers in his pockets and stood looking down at her. "I'll...let you get to work, then."

He took a few steps toward the door and then turned around. "Are you going to be okay?"

"Please, Luke." Her voice was wobbly, as though she was about to cry. "Please just go."

How could he leave her in that condition? But he was obviously causing her distress. Without another word he reached the door and let himself out.

All the way back to his condo he tried to figure out what had happened. Had he misread the signals? Or had he been too rough? All he knew was that the crack inside him that had started letting light in sealed up tighter than ever before. The world seemed darker again.

KRISTEN STEPPED OUT OF the shower, exhausted from sobbing. As she dried off, she stilled in front of the mirror. Slowly, she opened the towel and studied her reflection. Her body was the same body she'd had since maturing. Except for the long, ugly scars that ran along her right side and under her right arm and breast. And the fake nipple that felt nothing and did nothing.

Mastectomy had saved her life. And reconstruction gave her some semblance of normalcy. Every day she reminded herself how lucky she was to be alive.

And she was, but…

She closed the towel back to hide the disfigurement and felt her face crumple.

If *she* thought it was disgusting after all these months of getting used to it, what would a man think of it?

Coward! She'd never know if she couldn't work up the courage to actually let a man see her.

Yes, she knew Luke had probably seen worse. He was a doctor. He served in Afghanistan. He'd probably seen all kinds of horrific disfigurements. Surely he'd be okay with it. And she'd handle any questions he might have with simple honesty.

That's what she'd told herself in his Jeep all the way back to her condo. And when he'd kissed her. And when he'd come down on top of her on the sofa. Right up until he'd lifted her T-shirt and touched her. Then she'd frozen. Panicked that he'd be disgusted. Or pity her. Or both.

Oh, God, poor Luke. He didn't understand. And she'd been too humiliated to explain. How could she have done that to him? She should go to him and ask his forgiveness and tell him.

But, maybe it was better this way. He'd be back in Afghanistan in a few weeks, and she'd be back in San Diego.

She'd just be a memory of some weird girl he met in Hawaii.

And he'd always be a reminder of what might have been.

5

"So," AMY WHISPERED to Kristen as they were both waiting for customers' drink orders at the bar. "How'd it go this afternoon with Captain Mysterious?" She wiggled her brows.

If Kristen hadn't avoided her gaze and bitten her bottom lip, Amy might have thought she didn't hear her. The Beach Boys' "Kokomo" was playing loudly over the speakers, but, still… "Hey, what is it?"

Kristen turned to her with red-rimmed eyes. "I ruined everything."

"Oh, no! What happened?"

Kristen shook her head. "I can't talk about it here." She grabbed her drinks and placed them on her tray. "We'll talk after work?" At Amy's nod, she threw a grateful look over her shoulder and took off for her section.

Amy picked up her tray of cocktails, swung it over her head and sauntered over to her waiting customers.

She turned to the next table, ready to take their order and stopped cold. Kekoa.

"What are you doing here?" she blurted out. Her reaction this morning had been completely spontaneous, but she had no regrets.

"Thought I'd have another of those Sneaky Tikis I made for me."

Yeah, right, and she was a MENSA member. She narrowed her eyes and stuck a hand on her hip. "What do you really want?"

He folded his arms, drew a quick breath that expanded his already broad chest and let it out on a huff. "Okay. We need to talk."

"I get a break in—" she checked the huge beer clock on the wall above the bar "—about two hours. Come back then."

"No. We'll speak now."

"Look, you can't just—"

"I spoke with your shift manager. He's agreed to give you fifteen minutes if I buy a drink and wait until you clear your tables. So, I'll wait."

Amy blinked over at her boss. Really? No one ever got more than their usual break under Frank's watchful eye. How had Kekoa managed that? She looked back at him. He still had his arms crossed and sat as if made of stone.

A shiver of something more than just physical attraction tingled through her. As much as she craved her independence and wouldn't dream of letting a man run

her life—been there, done that—there was something…
thrilling about Kekoa making special arrangements just
to speak with her. It's not as if he'd come lumbering in
and tried to drag her out forcibly. "Okay." She tossed
her hair back. "One Sneaky Tiki coming up."

Within fifteen minutes, all her tables were taken care
of and Frank gestured for her to take a break. Kekoa
was waiting for her as she came out of the ladies' room
from freshening her makeup. He blocked the entry to
the restroom alcove as if he feared she might slip away.
As if she would.

"Could we talk outside?" He gestured toward the
side door.

"Sure." Though she was nervous, she smiled and led
the way to a tiny garden with a humpback-whale foun-
tain and a cement bench tucked away under palms and
surrounded by bright-colored hibiscus. She sat, crossed
her legs and bounced one back and forth.

Kekoa paced in front of her. He cleared his throat.
"As the son of a chief, it is my duty to make an alliance
with the daughter of a respectable island family."

Amy stopped bouncing her leg. "And you're telling
me this because…?"

"I've sought guidance from the gods, but I've been
given no resolution to my dilemma."

"Your…dilemma?"

He glanced at her as he continued pacing. "You
must understand that you're completely inappropriate
for me."

Amy straightened her spine and crossed her arms. "Must I?"

He stopped pacing and faced her. "Yes. My...attraction to you isn't something I'm happy about. You're—" he waved his arm up and down her figure "—a cocktail waitress. If we're going to continue this affair, I'll be going against my *Ohana,* my honor, even my best interests."

Fury struck her core like lightning and she shot up from her seat. "What on earth makes you think I'd continue anything with you, you arrogant—"

He took hold of her shoulders and pressed his mouth to hers. She remained stiff in his arms, her mouth shut while he cupped the back of her head and moved his lips over hers, enticing, cajoling, until finally she opened to him.

Triumphant, he plunged his tongue in to claim her and deepened the kiss until he was devouring her. With a rough groan, his mouth slid down to capture her neck and nibble up behind her ear.

Amy's bones seemed to have dissolved. She clung to his shirtfront and leaned her head back to give him what he wanted. Wait. Why was she giving him what he wanted? Just because her body wanted it, too? That was no good reason. Not after he'd insulted her so completely. She wasn't expecting a proposal of marriage— God forbid—but she at least expected the man she had an affair with to *want* to want her. She shoved away from him and headed back toward the side entrance. Surely her fifteen minutes were up by now.

"Amy!" His voice was husky behind her and he made a grab for her arm but missed.

Opening the door, she swung back to face him. "You might try improving your come-on line, sweetie. Telling a woman she's 'inappropriate' is a real turnoff." Spinning on her four-inch heels, she strode through the door and made her way back to Frank and her section.

AFTER THE BAR CLOSED for the night, Kristen changed clothes in the restroom as usual, eager to get out of her heels.

As they headed outside, Kristen opened her mouth to ask Amy for a ride, too exhausted to contemplate walking home. She'd left her mangled bike in her condo to deal with another day.

But chained to a light post in the parking lot beside Amy's Toyota was a brand-new two-toned seven-speed women's cruiser bicycle. With a big red bow taped on the seat and the key to the lock taped under the bow.

Luke.

Clearly giving her the bike this way meant he hadn't wanted to communicate with her. She didn't blame him.

She thought she'd cried her last tear in the shower this evening, but...no.

Thank goodness for Amy. She was the older sister Kristen had never had. Kristen cried on her shoulder and Amy listened and sympathized without offering advice. Kristen was close to her mom, but sex and her body issues weren't something she could talk about over a long-distance phone call.

When Kristen brought up the subject of Kekoa, Amy laughed it off, claiming that at thirty, she was too old to make the same mistake twice, and that she was over that silly infatuation.

Kristen didn't believe her. But she knew about Amy's ex, and the part about making the same mistake bothered her. Kekoa would never hurt a woman.

The next two days, Kristen's routine remained the same. Up at six, on the water with Kekoa by seven, diving, snapping photos of the humpbacks, corals, tropical fish, all the exquisite sea life Hawaiian waters had to offer.

Friday afternoon she sat at the kitchen table uploading the day's photos into her laptop. Still nothing screamed *winner* at her. No single photo seemed unique enough to enter. And the contest deadline was only two weeks away.

She tried not to question her decision to come here. But she'd spent a lot of money on this venture. What if she failed? The idea of losing had always been some abstract possibility far in the future. But it loomed in front of her now, like a tropical storm threatening to destroy her dream.

Yet, if she were honest with herself, it wasn't the prospect of losing this contest that made her world seem full of ominous clouds. No, she'd weighed that outcome carefully before signing those loan papers with her grandmother. And every time, her conclusion had always been, better to fail than to never have tried.

Though the contest was a niggling worry, her most miserable thoughts always centered on Luke.

What must he think of her? She hadn't seen him at all. Not on the beach, or in the lobby. He was probably avoiding her. And who could blame him?

She deleted the worst photos, sorted the rest of what she'd taken this morning into groups and then clicked on the folder she'd created titled Luke. Several photos appeared on her screen. Though he hadn't liked it, she'd taken a few of him on the boat and in the souvenir shop while his attention had been elsewhere. His quiet shyness drew her to him more than any charming come-on.

The fact that he was so good-looking only added fuel to the fire. His angular jaw contrasted nicely with his slightly turned-up nose. And though his brown hair was cut short, it still managed to curl just a bit on the ends, with one lock falling over his forehead that made her want to reach out and sweep it back.

Pain stabbed her chest. Thinking of him, or rather, her behavior with him, ate away at her peace and happiness. She'd tried to call him both yesterday and this morning to thank him for the bike, and his cell phone had gone straight to voice mail. She certainly understood why he wouldn't want to speak with her.

She was the one who had initiated everything. She'd introduced herself, asked him to dinner, invited him to spend the day with her on the boat. And longed for his kiss. Oh, his kiss. She'd dated plenty in high school. She'd had a boyfriend for a while in college. But she'd never been kissed the way Luke kissed her. It'd been as if he poured his soul into his kiss.

And then, she'd stopped him. Without explanation. And the worst of it was she hadn't meant to. It'd been a reflex that had surprised her as much as him. But the damage was done. He probably thought she was the worst tease ever. She couldn't stand for him to think that she was only playing some cruel game with him.

Well, she wasn't giving up. She grabbed her cell phone, pulled up his number and hit Dial.

"Andrews," Luke's deep voice answered on the second ring, but it sounded gravelly, as if he hadn't used it in a while.

"Luke?"

Silence on the other end. Then finally, "Kristen?"

"Yeah. Hi. I wanted to thank you for the bicycle. That was totally not necessary."

She heard some fumbling with the phone, and then, "Least I could do."

"Fact is, I love it. It's beautiful. So…thank you." Her words trailed off and she cringed. Could she be any more lame?

Silence.

"Um, how are you doing?"

"I been jus' fine."

He didn't sound just fine. His words were slurred

and his Texas drawl was more pronounced. And the flippant tone didn't sound like the Luke she'd gotten to know either. Was he drunk? At three in the afternoon? "Listen, Luke. We should talk."

The silence lasted so long this time she thought maybe he'd left the phone or hung up. Then she heard, "Doan think that'd be a good idea." And he clicked off.

Kristen stared at her cell. Something was wrong. It sounded crazy when she'd only known the guy a few days, but she felt it in her gut. And it was her fault.

She darted out the door and punched the elevator button, all the while trying to picture seeing him on his balcony that night. How many stories up had his condo been? And how many balconies over from the lobby? Counting in her head, she stepped into the elevator and hit the button for the fifth floor. If she was wrong, she'd go up and down each floor and knock on every door if she had to.

Once on the fifth floor, she went to the third door on the side facing the ocean. She closed her eyes and took a deep breath. There were so many ways this could go horribly wrong. The least of which was some stranger answered the door and she had to explain herself.

Letting out her breath, she opened her eyes and straightened her spine. And knocked.

And waited. Maybe the occupant had a normal job and was still at work. She knocked again, a little louder this time. After waiting another few seconds, she moved to the next door down the hall when she heard a thump and a crash from inside the condo.

"Luke?" She banged on the door, good manners gone. "Luke, are you all right?" She used the heel of her hand to pound this time. Midpound, the door swung open.

Luke squinted at her. "I told you I'm fine."

My God, he looked awful. Unshaven, disheveled, gaunt. She swallowed. "Can I please come in?"

He shifted weight from one bare foot to the other, then headed into the condo, leaving the door wide-open.

As she followed him in, he righted a small table between the sofa and a recliner and picked up a lamp and put it on the table. Then he gathered up empty takeout cartons, a couple of beer cans and trash. "Have a seat." He disappeared into the kitchen.

The condo was utilitarian. Neat except for the general area around the recliner. But the place was dark and stuffy. The blinds were drawn, the curtains shut. She marched to the balcony, drew back the curtains and pulled up the blinds, and threw open the balcony doors. Fresh sea air and the sound of crashing waves filled the room.

"Make yourself at home."

She swung around to find Luke glaring at her, his hands on his slim hips. He wore nothing except a pair of khaki cargo shorts and a silver chain with dog tags. She drew in a ragged breath. Dog tags that lay on a bare chest sprinkled with light brown hair that tapered down to a narrow line over abdomen muscles so defined that *six-pack* was an understatement.

"I wanted to apologize for the other night."

He glanced away, his upper body twisting to scan the condo. "No need. I'm probably the one who should apologize." He squeezed his eyes closed and pinched the bridge of his nose.

"It wasn't you at all. I—"

He swayed on his feet and stumbled back, stopping himself on the arm of the sofa. Kristen darted forward to catch him, or help somehow, but he gestured for her to stay away and lowered himself onto the sofa.

"Luke, what's going on?"

"Nothin', I'm fine." But he laid his head back along the top of the sofa. A dog whined and for the first time she noticed the tan shepherd with black ears lying beside the sofa.

"What's with your dog?"

"Nothing. It's just a stray. I'm going to take him to the shelter."

"Oh." She sat beside Luke and placed her hand on his arm. "Please talk to me. I just need to know you're okay. Then I'll go away and never bother you again."

"Kristen." He lifted his head and met her gaze. His eyes were bloodshot. Just being this close to him made her body ache in all the right ways. "It's nothin'. I couldn't sleep, so I took a perfectly safe sleeping pill." He shrugged. "Or maybe two."

Her chest squeezed tight. He'd mentioned having trouble sleeping the night of their first date. But was it worse because of what she'd done to him? He was still slurring his words, maybe he was loose enough to talk to her. But, maybe she shouldn't take advantage of his weakened state. "Why can't you sleep?"

With a sigh, he leaned forward, rested his elbows on his knees, and scrubbed his face with his hands. "It's these damn nightmares," he said, digging his fingers into his scalp.

"Nightmares about…"

"The hospital in Kabul." Still resting his head in his hands, he slanted his gaze to her and his face scrunched up. "I can't save them, Kristen. I can't."

"Oh, Luke." She longed to pull him into her arms, but she settled for placing a hand on his shoulder. His skin was hot, almost feverish. She wished she knew how to help him, but it sounded as if he might need more than a friendly ear. "You need to talk to someone about it. Someone who knows how to deal with these things."

He blinked and then scowled. "I'm dealing with it."

She removed her hand, folded her arms and raised a dubious brow. He broke eye contact and flopped against the back of the couch again. "So, now you know I'm okay, you can go."

She straightened. So, that was it? He couldn't—or wouldn't—acknowledge there was a problem, much less forgive her. But she still wanted…something.

She propelled herself off the couch. "Come snorkeling with me in the morning. You never got to go, and I've been wanting to go back to Molokini."

He studied her, his jaw shifting to the left a fraction. "What's going on here, Kristen? What happened the other night?"

"I, uh..." Huh. *Be careful what you wish for.* She'd hoped she wouldn't have to explain. If she told him, he'd look at her differently. As though she was some invalid. Or freak. Despite the fact he was a doctor. Or maybe even because of it. He probably knew exactly what a post-op mastectomy looked like. But he was still a man. A man who could be turned off by her scars. Yet she didn't want to lie to him either. "I just wasn't ready." It was her turn to shrug. "I thought I was, but... it's been a long time."

He studied her with narrowed eyes and then nodded. "Okay." The muscles in his arm flexed as he scratched the back of his head, then his hand fell to his thigh. It was such an utterly masculine gesture, an utterly masculine pose, slumped on the couch with his legs spread wide. "So, what do you want from me?"

She pictured herself curled up in his arms, snuggling and kissing. She wanted that—desperately. Just that. If he tried to do more, would she be able to let him? "Could we maybe take it slow?"

"What's your definition of slow? Do I give it a few days, a week? We've only got a couple weeks left here, right?"

She nodded. "True. I don't know either." She bit her lip. Maybe she should just fling her clothes off right now and—

"I'm sorry. Never mind. How about we just be friends?"

She blinked. Just friends? "Uh… Okay."

He pushed off the sofa, took her elbow and guided her to the door. "You go get that winning photo, okay? And I'm—I'm glad I met you." He leaned in and caught her gaze, hesitated and then gave her a peck on the cheek.

She gave him a wobbly smile. She should be happy that they'd worked things out, right? And she was. Friends. They would be friends. And friends did lots of fun things together. "So, you'll come snorkeling with me in the morning?"

He shook his head and opened his mouth to say something, and then shut it again. The corners of his mouth curved up, but his eyes still looked sad. He nodded. "Okay."

"Good." He was right. There were only a couple weeks left here. This was probably for the best. She'd be grateful for this relationship, whatever it was, or turned out to be. All she knew was, she wasn't ready for it to be over.

6

As Luke shaved the next morning, he took a long look at himself in the mirror. The man staring back was a stranger. What was he doing? Taking sleeping pills? Hiding from life? That wasn't like him. What would he have done if Kristen hadn't forced her way into his condo? He wasn't sure he wanted to know the answer to that. He shoved away from the sink and stepped into the shower.

Still, he should've told her no. How could he spend the day with her and pretend he just wanted to be friends? And why had he suggested that in the first place? *You know why, Andrews.* Yesterday, when she'd tried to explain, the fear in her eyes had demolished him. He'd felt like a jerk for even asking. So, they'd just be friends.

The damned earrings were sitting on his bedside table, mocking him. He'd never been an impulsive person. And this was exactly why. He could stroll over to that volleyball game down on the beach and get himself in the game. In more ways than one. Find a hot girl in a bikini... But he'd never been a real ladies' man. He was shy, always had been the quiet type. His sister called him introverted.

All he knew was he found it difficult to initiate contact. Maybe if he had several drinks in him. He could hit one of the local bars, but that hadn't ended the way he'd hoped at Tradewinds.

Right now, he had a date to go snorkeling. He probably shouldn't have agreed to see her today, but telling Kristen no would've felt like denying himself sustenance.

Within ten minutes he'd thrown on swim trunks and a T-shirt and was driving Kristen to the marina. Maybe he shouldn't have brought the dog, but Luke couldn't bear to leave the poor guy alone in that condo all morning like last time. The mutt seemed pretty happy, sticking his head out, his ears flying and his tongue lolling out to the side.

The bright sun hurt Luke's eyes, even through his sunglasses. But it felt warm on his skin and just being outside after so many days cooped up in the condo sent his senses into overload—the solid feel of the wheel beneath his hands, the briny scent of the ocean, the rough growl of the Jeep's engine and the dappled shadows cast by tall palms lining the road.

His heart raced when he looked at Kristen sitting beside him.

The wind blew her hair all around, and he expected her to be grinning, maybe even throw her hands up and squeal as they zipped around a tight curve. But when he glanced at her she was staring at him, her usual smile missing. What was she thinking behind such a serious expression? Wouldn't a friend simply ask her?

Friends. It was crazy. He'd suggested it as a way out for both of them. Had she not seen that?

A song about a sponge named Bob started playing. Kristen dug around in her purse, pulled out her cell and answered. "Hi, Amy."

Seconds of silence were interspersed with "Yeah," or "Uh-huh" or "Oh, that's tomorrow?" Then she said, "Okay, I will, bye." And clicked off.

"Guess what?" She beamed at him.

"What?"

"There's a luau tomorrow night for Valentine's Day. Have you ever been to a luau? I have to work, just during the show, but I'll be off after. I've always wanted to see one. This should be so fun. It's going to be right there on Kamaole Beach. Want to go?"

He couldn't help grinning at her enthusiasm. "Sure."

She squealed and lunged across the gearshift to give him a quick hug.

For that moment, speeding down the highway, Luke felt like a king.

He pulled into the marina and parked, and once on the boat, Luke's blond-haired, blue-eyed *friend* stripped down to her short, black wet suit. The T-back was about as revealing as it got. It occurred to him he'd never seen Kristen in a bathing suit. Which was odd. Girls in bikinis were to Maui beaches what cattle were to his West Texas hometown.

They were everywhere.

The water must be too cold at the depth she was diving.

"I haven't been to the Molokini Crater since you were with us last time," she said as Kekoa shut off the engine and drifted into the concave side of the formation. "There was a crown-of-thorns starfish I tried to photograph that might just win me the contest, but then my hook broke loose before I could get a picture." She lifted the lid of a storage box and pulled out fins, vests and snorkeling masks.

"You're going back where the current almost swept you away?"

She stopped and tilted her head, frowning. "Of course. I haven't got a winning photo yet."

"But…" Luke wanted to order her not to go down there again. It was too dangerous. No contest was worth her life. Didn't she realize how fragile life was? He couldn't count the number of kids he'd been talking with one day and recording their time of death the next. He saw their faces, dozens of young men and women, as he zipped up the body bags.

"Luke." A soft hand rubbed his arm. At the contact he opened his eyes and saw the most beautiful, sky-blue eyes staring up at him. He wasn't in Kabul. He was out in the bright sun, on a boat bobbing up and down on sparkling turquoise water. He'd had another flashback. They were getting out of control. He apologized as he took the vest Kristen held for him.

There really wasn't a graceful way to get into the water while wearing swim fins, but Kristen made it look easy. After some basic instructions on snorkeling, Luke sat on the edge of the boat and shoved off. In one splash he was immersed in cool, clear water. It was exhilarating, refreshing, reviving.

Once he put in his mouthpiece and lowered his face into the water, he found himself in a magical world. Schools of fish—hundreds probably—with brilliant orange stripes, vivid yellows and neon greens, darted past and back again. There was pink-and-purple coral and giant sea turtles. Far in the distance, Kristen pointed to a couple of white-tipped sharks minding their own business.

When he looked back at Kristen, their gazes locked and it was as if they needed no words to communicate. This world, a world she spent most of her days exploring, was beyond words. How to describe the beauty, the simplicity, the peace down here?

But he didn't have to. He stared into Kristen's eyes and he knew that she knew. She understood. Because she felt the same way. He knew that, too.

He wasn't sure how long they swam and dove and explored. He admitted that when he reflected on this experience it would always seem like a time out of time.

When they surfaced and climbed back on the *Ho`opono,* he let her board first. Setting a foot on the bottom rung, he clasped her waist with both hands and lifted her up the ladder. She turned back to him with a look of hot, intense longing. He couldn't have made himself let go of her then if he'd had a gun to his head. For a second he thought she might lean down and kiss him. Or what if he slid his hands up along her rib cage to cup her breasts?

He closed his eyes and let his hands drop. She'd made it clear she needed time. Time they didn't have.

While Kristen got into her scuba equipment, Kekoa showed Luke the basics of running the boat, the radio and emergency codes. Then Kekoa pulled on his fins and what he called a BCD—a black vest like Kristen's, only his was bigger and thicker. It was a buoyancy compensator, Kristen explained, that carried an extra oxygen tank with pockets for cameras and ropes. This was state-of-the-art scuba gear.

It looked heavy and Luke rushed over to help Kristen lift hers up onto her shoulders and push her arms through. It swallowed her up, made her look so tiny, so…vulnerable.

She looked over her shoulder at him. "Thank you."

Her smile was still missing. He could swear he saw desire in her eyes. If he lowered his head just a few inches…

He patted her shoulders and stepped away. She blinked, and then followed Kekoa to the boat's edge.

Luke wanted to plead with her not to go. Reach for her, hold her and—yeah, if he did that, he wouldn't stop there.

Before he was ready, she pulled her mask over her eyes and nose, stuck her regulator in her mouth, waved goodbye and rolled off into the water. As magic as the underwater world had been mere minutes before, it now morphed into a dark and dangerous place. He wanted to snatch the line attached to the boat that she used to descend, and yank it back up. He felt short of breath and his skin went clammy. If anything happened to her...

His intellect told him panic was irrational, but the shaking and the flashes of disturbing images didn't go away.

He paced the length of the boat, time ticking sluggishly by. The dog whined and followed him, back and forth. Every fifteen minutes Luke checked the line for signs of movement, and then he'd go back to pacing the boat. This was torture. There was nothing he could do. It was the same in Kabul. So much seemed beyond his ability to make a difference. That's what he couldn't stand, the helplessness.

After what seemed like hours, but was probably less than one, the line started twitching and finally—God, finally—Kristen surfaced.

Once she got halfway up the ladder, Luke gripped her under her arms and hauled her up on deck. Despite her bulky BCD and the mask on top of her head, he held her tight against him and buried his nose in her dripping hair. He felt her arms go around him, her hands rubbing his back and her breath puffing against the front of his T-shirt.

"Luke?" She tried to pull back, but he tightened his arms. He wasn't ready to let go. Gradually he loosened his hold and she lifted her face.

Kekoa had discreetly disappeared into his cabin, and the dog followed, leaving them alone on deck. It took everything in Luke not to kiss her. He made himself smile and step away. "Did you get your photo?"

She grinned. "I did. I can't wait to get it uploaded and see how it turned out."

"I'd like to see all your pictures sometime."

"No time like the present. Want to grab some sandwiches and take them back to my place? All my work is on my laptop."

He must be a glutton for punishment. But Kristen's photography was such a big part of who she was, and he wanted to know all about it. "Sure."

All he had to do was manage to keep his hands off her for the rest of the afternoon.

KRISTEN HANDED THE BAG with the sandwiches to Luke and fished in her backpack for her key. Memories of the last time she'd tried to unlock this door with Luke standing beside her invaded her senses.

She closed her eyes and drew a deep breath. The air between them seemed charged with—she didn't know what to call it. Maybe for him it was just awkward. But she'd felt it on the boat this morning, too. Need. Desire.

Maybe it was a case of vacation fling fever. It'd been years since she'd had sex. But only recently had she felt in any way sexual. For Luke, though, getting some booty had to have been the main goal of this tropical vacation. With all the beautiful women running around in bikinis, he could have his choice.

So, why wasn't he—wait, maybe he had, did, was. He didn't seem like a player, but she barely knew the guy. He could be seeing someone, or even many some-ones, and she wouldn't know it. Maybe that's why he'd been so quick to suggest they only be friends.

How depressing.

Shaking off her erratic thoughts, she found her key, unlocked the door and ushered Luke in. He set the food on the kitchen table while she opened her laptop and clicked it on.

"You want a soda? Or water?" She had to brush past him to get to the fridge.

"Sure."

She grabbed two cans of cola, set them on the table with their sandwiches and then sat at her laptop to open her Maui folder. He pulled a chair around next to her and sat, leaning in close to see the screen. She was hy-peraware of his nearness, of his faint but distinctive co-logne and of the last time he'd been here. Oh, no. Her face heated.

"Here you go." She shoved the laptop in front of him and reached across the table for the cold soda can.

Resisting the urge to roll it across her forehead, she popped the top and took a long swallow.

"Wow, these are spectacular," he said as he scrolled through the pictures.

"You'd have to be pretty incompetent to take a bad picture in Maui, but...I don't think there's anything really unique. You've seen the pictures in the *Geographic Universe,* right? They always have the most amazing photos."

Still staring at the screen and clicking on photos, he nodded. "I know what you mean. But still, yours are exquisite."

She'd love to photograph him right now, with his expression of deep concentration and the way he pursed his lips and twitched them to the left. It was so unique. So him. She darted into the bedroom, returned with her Nikon and snapped a few candid pics before he noticed what she was up to.

When he looked up and saw her, he grimaced and put a hand in front of his face. "That won't win you any contests."

"These are just for me." She smiled and lowered her camera. "I should get some of your dog." They'd dropped him off at Luke's condo before coming here.

"He's not my dog." Luke was turned in the chair, his legs spread, one arm resting along the back of the chair, the other on the table. Nothing special about the pose, but he wore a very tiny smile, and he seemed so relaxed. Even on the boat, he'd been tense, almost remote. She moved closer and swept that mischievous lock of hair off his forehead, then raised the camera and snapped another picture.

When she looked up from the camera's image display, he'd lost his smile and the tenseness had returned to his features. And in his dark eyes was that barely caged need she'd sensed earlier.

And she felt the same. A desire to be in his arms and to be kissed and, yes, even more. An ache throbbed deep inside, between her thighs, insistent, demanding to be filled. By him.

Feeling deprived of oxygen, she took in a long, quivering breath and saw his gaze shift from her eyes to her chest. As if they'd been touched, her nipples responded, tightening to the point of pain—or rather, her left one did. The reconstructed one on the right did nothing, felt nothing. Thank goodness she'd changed into shorts and a T-shirt at the marina. He wouldn't be able to tell one breast was different than the other.

Even now, six months after the reconstruction, she always wore clothes that covered the scars. Their redness had faded to pink, and the swelling was almost nonexistent. But they still weren't a pretty sight.

They never would be.

Like a cold splash of water, her desire was doused, leaving only a hissing smoky mess.

She latched on to the nearest distraction. Lunch. If she couldn't satisfy one hunger, she'd fill another. "Man, I'm starving, aren't you?" Grabbing a sandwich off the table, she sat in the chair farthest from Luke, unwrapped and bit into the pita bread with gusto.

Luke swiveled to face her across the table and reached for the other sandwich. But his attention was on her laptop screen. He clicked again and again and finally said, "Is this your mom? You look like her."

Her mom? There shouldn't be any pictures of her mother in the Maui folder. What file had he opened? No! She jumped up and slammed the laptop closed.

"What the..." Luke leaned back, his hands in the air at his shoulders. He looked at her as if she were crazy.

She tried to make herself laugh, but it probably sounded more like a hyena. "Those are my personal pictures." She shrugged. "You know, just dumb, embarrassing family stuff." Okay, that was pretty much true, if not the whole truth.

He stared at her, frowning. "Yeah, sure. I'm sorry." He lowered his hands and rubbed them on his thighs. "I shouldn't have opened the folder without permission."

Kristen couldn't think of a thing to say. A part of her wanted to explain. But there'd be no going back once he knew. Still, what's the worst that could happen? She pictured herself telling him. He'd look at her with pity and mumble some excuse about having to be somewhere.

"You know—" Luke glanced at his watch "—I better get going." He stood.

Kristen blinked. "Oh, uh, fine." She got to her feet, still feeling she should explain everything, but she just couldn't force the words past her lips. While she quarreled with herself, he had already made his way to the door. She followed, telling him goodbye as if in a daze.

After the door closed she stood there, a sharp pain slamming into her temples. She gripped her head and squeezed her eyes closed. Now what had she done?

7

"MAI TAI OR A BLUE HAWAII, ma'am?" Kristen offered her tray of cocktails to the older couple in the front row.

Every year, South Shore Cruises hosted a luau for their customers and hired Tradewinds to cater traditional luau foods and drinks. Roasted pig, *Lomilomi* salmon, long rice, *Haupia,* a coconut pudding and, of course, poi.

The touring company had set up a small stage in the sand, brought in tiki torches to light the beach and lined up dozens of seating pads for their customers to sit on. As the native dancers in their grass skirts and feather headdresses took the stage, Kristen saw Amy serving the food. The drums pounded and the dancers in their grass skirts and feather headdresses mesmerized the audience with their hips swaying and shaking.

The luau was also open to the public for a fee. But Luke hadn't shown up.

As she served Mai Tais and Blue Hawaiis, Kristen

kept checking his balcony. No light showed through his sliding door. A couple of times the hairs on her neck rose and she'd glance at his balcony. But she never saw anything.

The fire dancers ended the night's entertainment with breathtaking feats, twirling flaming sticks and tossing them back and forth. By ten the families with children and most of the older folks packed up and strolled back to their accommodation.

That's when the real party began.

Kristen happily clocked out, with Amy right behind her. The stage was taken apart and removed and a bonfire was lit. Rock music blared from car speakers and ice chests of beer appeared from the tailgates of trucks.

Amy changed from her grass skirt into a bikini and flirted with a couple of guys from Ohio. Whatever had happened between her and Kekoa was definitely over. As Kristen surveyed the crowd it seemed as though everyone around the bonfire was paired up. Some had already started kissing and snuggling.

An ache jabbed her chest. She grabbed a beer, twisted the top off and took a swig.

Luke hadn't come.

She took another long drink of the cold beer, feeling it hit her empty stomach. She'd had three strikes with Luke and she was out. That thought needed another long swallow. How had it come to this?

When she'd first arrived in Maui she'd planned to

have a sexual adventure. Go crazy and enjoy life to the fullest.

Her hair had grown back, she'd regained the weight she'd lost and her strength had returned. And she'd finally begun to feel like a sexual being again after two and a half long years.

Since most of the guys she met here were only looking for one thing, she'd assumed it'd be easy to have a fun fling.

But the guys had all seemed like boys. Silly, immature. She just hadn't been attracted. She wanted something…more.

Wow, these were small bottles of beer. She grabbed another, twisted off the cap and gulped down several swallows.

So, did that make her a prude? Even before facing death at twenty-one she'd never been the kind to enjoy a quick roll in the sack. She'd had a steady boyfriend in college. And that was about it for sexual experience. Not that she was ready for marriage. But before sex, she wanted romance, a connection.

Luke.

She took another sip.

He wasn't like the young men she'd met here. He understood what it was to look into the abyss and feel it sucking you in. Even before she'd known about him serving in Afghanistan she'd sensed that dark side of him. The something more she wanted was with Luke.

If she wanted that—and if it wasn't already too

late—she'd have to tell him the truth. She'd have to risk his pity. And his rejection. So, what else was new? she scoffed, finishing off the second beer.

So, what was she going to do, remain celibate the rest of her life? If not, she'd have to tell some man, someday. Did she want a full life, or didn't she? To live, to really live, meant experiencing everything, the good, the bad, the ugly.

She pushed off the sand and made her way over to Amy. "Hey."

Her friend met her gaze, frowned and jumped to her feet. "What is it?"

Kristen lifted her chin. "I'm going to Luke's."

Amy's brows rose. "You go, girl!" She held her hand up for Kristen to wait. "But tell Captain Mysterious, if he hurts you, I'll feed his man parts to the sharks."

Kristen grinned, the image taking her mind off her nervousness. She hugged her friend, and then took off at a jog away from the beach, across the street and all the way to the front of her building. Pausing, she looked up at Luke's balcony.

A shadow moved and then a dark figure appeared, lit only by the extended light from the flickering flames of the bonfire. He stared down at her and she whispered his name. Without waiting to see what he might do, she entered the lobby and then the elevator. She punched the button for the fifth floor and when it stopped there, she strode to Luke's door and knocked before she had time to lose her courage.

She was out of breath and trembling when he opened the door. "Luke," she gasped, trying to catch her breath.

He took her hand and led her inside, then quietly closed the door behind her. His condo was dark. But she could see his tall form in front of her. "What's wrong?" He sounded suspicious, but she could also hear the fatigue in his deep voice.

The dog's cold nose nudged her thigh and she startled, and then petted the animal.

"Go lie down, dog," Luke ordered, and the dog obeyed.

"Luke." She laid her palms flat on his chest. His bare chest. His skin was hot. Instinctively she ran her hands up over his shoulders and back down to rest at the waistband of his jeans. She heard his swift intake of breath. "Luke, I don't want to be just friends." She rose up on her toes and kissed under his jaw. Mmm… She inhaled his clean scent.

"Kristen." He turned his head away, kept his arms at his sides. "I don't—"

"I know. I screwed up so many times." She kissed down his neck to his collarbone and she felt him swallow. "But if you give me one more chance, I'll make it up to you."

He didn't say anything and she raised to meet him and waited. She'd gotten used to his moments of silence before he spoke. She admired that he thought about things before he answered. It was not one of her talents.

He made a sound deep in his throat, cupped her face

in his hands and lowered his mouth to hers. His lips moved over hers with strength and longing. Her nervousness melted away and her hands roamed to the back of his neck and crept into his hair. He pulled her closer and deepened the kiss and she whimpered, surrendering all.

But he stilled, his mouth leaving hers. His hands dropped and he reached up and took her hands off the back of his head.

"Luke, please."

"Shh." He stepped back, and kept backing up, leading her by her hands to the bedroom. "You had me with the grass skirt and the flower behind your ear."

She smiled, only now realizing she'd forgotten to change from her work outfit. "You like hula girls, huh?"

"I like this hula girl." His voice was low and soft.

The bedroom was even darker, which made it a little easier for Kristen to get through what she did next. Swaying her hips as she walked, she let go of his hands and slowly slipped her T-shirt off over her head. "Shall I leave the skirt on?"

The back of his legs bumped the end of the bed and he dropped down. "No." He clutched her waist and pulled her between his thighs. "Don't leave anything on."

"Yes, sir." She saluted, then hooked her thumbs into the band of the skirt and her panties at the same time, shoved them both down to her ankles and stepped out of them.

Immediately his hands wandered down her hips to her thighs, and around to her bottom. His mouth landed on her stomach and she gripped the back of his head. He continued running his hands down her thighs to behind her knees. Then up between her legs. With a bit of urging from him she brought one foot up to the bed beside him.

As his mouth and tongue caressed down her stomach into her blond curls, his fingers slid between her thighs and stroked her folds. He made sure to pause at her swollen clit and rub with just the right amount of pressure. With each stroke his speed increased until he finally slipped a finger inside her. She moaned and thought herself in heaven.

But Luke had only begun. His mouth replaced his thumb, leaving his fingers free to concentrate on the speed and depth of their thrusts.

Her hips pushed forward as he lathed and suckled, and she clutched his head as pleasure gave way to urgent need. Faster, harder, more. The sensation building, boiling... She threw her head back and cried out as the most exquisite, intense orgasm of her life shook her body.

Her knees buckled and she slumped in Luke's arms. He caught her and rolled until she lay beneath him on the bed, her arms flung above her.

With one arm beneath her, he lightly trailed his fingers up and down her abdomen and pressed gentle kisses along the edge of her bra. He purposely hadn't touched her breasts. Did he know and was avoiding them? How could he know? Maybe it was only because of her reaction the last time he'd tried. And he was letting her decide when to take that step.

Oh, Luke.

Drawing in a deep breath, she let it out on a sigh. She reached behind her, unhooked her bra and drew it off. Then she took his hand and hesitantly placed it over her right breast.

He cupped it and rubbed a finger over the nipple. His thumb curved beneath and his fingers curled around the side to cup it, then abruptly stilled.

Kristen squeezed her eyes closed, knowing what he felt. One scar ran around the nipple, and it was fairly tiny, but the other ran from under her arm to the underside of her reconstructed breast. Was he totally turned off now?

She felt his lips where his thumb had been, kissing down along her scar, and all the way around her breast. Then he caught her nipple and, though she couldn't feel it, she watched as he teased it with his tongue and gently sucked. She wasn't very big, but what she had, he lifted and kissed all around before cupping the left with his other hand and kissing between them, and across to her left breast.

She gasped and arched her back as he took her left nipple into his mouth. He flicked his tongue over the hardened, puckered tip and then drew it into his mouth tenderly. It was as if all the sensation she'd lost in her

GET 2 BOOKS

We'd like to send you two *Harlequin® Blaze®*
novels absolutely free. Accepting them puts you under
no obligation to purchase any more books.

HOW TO GET YOUR
2 FREE BOOKS AND 2 FREE GIFTS

1. Return the reply card today, and we'll send you two
   Harlequin Blaze novels, absolutely free! We'll even pay
   the postage!

2. Accepting free books places you under no obligation
   to buy anything, ever. Whatever you decide, the free
   books and gifts are yours to keep, free!

3. We hope that after receiving your free books you'll
   want to remain a subscriber, but the choice is yours—
   to continue or cancel, any time at all!

EXTRA BONUS

You'll also get two free mystery gifts!
(worth about $10)

FREE!

If offer card is missing, write to: The Reader Service, P.O. Box 1867, Buffalo, NY 14240-1867 or visit www.ReaderService.com

BUSINESS REPLY MAIL
FIRST-CLASS MAIL   PERMIT NO. 717   BUFFALO, NY

POSTAGE WILL BE PAID BY ADDRESSEE

THE READER SERVICE
PO BOX 1867
BUFFALO NY 14240-9952

NO POSTAGE
NECESSARY
IF MAILED
IN THE
UNITED STATES

right nipple had transferred to her left. Tiny spasms rippled inside her. She writhed and moaned beneath him as he kissed her breast.

Tears she couldn't stop slid down her temples.

He moved up and took her mouth in a kiss slow and deep while his hand caressed her breast. When he raised his head, his dark eyes studied her as he carefully swept a lock of hair from her face and tucked it behind her ear. He traced the shell of her ear with one finger, and then brushed the back of his fingers across her cheek.

Finally his gaze returned to her eyes. His chest rose and fell, his skin warming hers where he lay alongside her. But he didn't move otherwise. He truly was leaving each step of the lovemaking up to her. If only he knew how desperately she wanted him.

She planted a hand on his chest and pushed him to his back. The same hand ran down his muscled abs and over the zipper of his jeans. He grunted softly as she palmed his erection.

How patient he'd been with her, considering how rock hard he was. Carefully, she unbuttoned his jeans and slid the zipper down, pulling his briefs down along with them. He lifted his hips to allow her to tug them down, but snatched his wallet from the pocket before she yanked them all the way off.

When she returned her attention to his cock it stood straight up, the tip glistening. Other than running a hand along her spine, he lay still and quiet, his other arm folded behind his head.

She glanced at him, wanting to see his face as she encircled his hard length. His eyes widened and then closed as she gripped him and stroked up and back down. His jaw shifted to the left. She pumped him again and then bent forward to take him inside her mouth. He gasped and his hand shot out to cup her cheek. She sucked hard, then released him and used her tongue to tease the head. Before she could take him inside her mouth again, he stopped her. "Wait."

He opened his eyes and met her gaze, his brows lowered. "I'm not sure how long I can last." His voice was rough, full of emotion.

She nodded.

He reached for his wallet, pulled out a condom and rolled it on. She straddled his thighs and massaged his chest, rubbing his flat nipples. Taking her time, she rose up on her knees, positioned him at her entrance and sank slowly down. He groaned, his hips lifting, his hands cupping and squeezing her breasts.

She rocked her hips and he groaned again. She was stretched so tight and filled so deeply. His thumbs rubbed across her nipples as he pushed inside her to her core and then pulled out and thrust again. He closed his eyes and stilled.

She wanted to watch him as he came. So she rose up and sank onto him, repeating the move, faster.

"Kristen." His voice was strangled. His hands went

to her waist to still her, but she rode him hard until his face creased and his jaw tightened. He let out a hoarse cry and his fingers dug into her waist.

As she watched him, ripples of pleasure multiplied and burst in a powerful climax. She fell on his chest and closed her eyes. His heart beat strong and fast beneath her ear. She quickly wiped a lone tear off her cheek before it landed on his heated skin.

So many emotions washed over her, overwhelmed her like giant waves tumbling her to shore. Relief was huge. Confidence and happiness filled her, too. She didn't have to be afraid of sex anymore. But mostly she felt an abiding connection to Luke. Not just gratitude or admiration, although that was part of it. She felt a closeness to him she would never forget.

As Luke's breathing finally slowed, languor set in, changing his muscles to lead and weighing down his eyelids. With Kristen's warm, soft skin against his, all he wanted to do was keep her in his arms and sleep for a dozen years. He hadn't felt such contentment, such peace since he was a kid. He'd found the cure for his insomnia.

But only a jerk would fall asleep right after sex. Especially after what he'd discovered. "How long has it been since the mastectomy?"

He felt her tense. "Almost two years." Kristen's voice was soft and her breath warm against his chest. "The summer before my junior year in college I was going to spend the day diving with my dad. Except when I was putting on my wet suit I felt a lump."

Filled with awe for her, he held her a bit tighter. "How many centimeters?"

"Two-point-one."

He whistled his amazement. "How old were you? Twenty? Twenty-one?"

"Yes. The reconstruction was only nine months ago."

"Well, I'm no plastic surgeon, but I'd say they did a heck of a job."

She lifted up on her forearms, her brows drawn together. "You really weren't turned off by the scarring?"

"Do I seem that shallow to you?"

She blinked and shook her head. "No, it's just that, I hadn't..." She closed her eyes. "You're my first since... everything."

His throat tightened. "I'm...honored you decided to trust me."

"I just...worried it would feel weird. To a guy, I mean."

He frowned. "Maybe I should double-check." His hand slid around to cup her left breast.

She raised a dubious brow. "Wrong side, Einstein."

"Aah, my mistake." He cupped her right breast, but didn't let go of her left and assumed a thoughtful expression. "Hmm." He proceeded to gently knead them both, rubbing his thumbs over the tips. "Hmm."

She laughed and then moaned and Luke relished the

sound. "Ms. Turner, I stand by my original assessment." He caught her gaze and held it. "You have great tits."

The smile she flashed seemed to light up the room. Then she kissed him, short, sweet little smooches on the lips. He touched her face and turned a short kiss into a long one, coaxing her mouth to open and accept just a hint of his tongue. She moaned and dug her fingers into his scalp, taking everything he offered. After moments of unhurried kissing, she pulled away, pressed lingering kisses down his jaw and then nuzzled into his neck.

He used her distraction to take care of the condom and then roll her beneath him. "However, this may take extensive research." Cupping her breasts, he lowered his head and took one tight nipple into his mouth. While she gasped, he teased the other between his thumb and finger and then kissed all over both breasts.

Once he'd given thorough attention to both, and she was panting, he moved over her, spread her thighs with his knees and kissed his way down to her stomach and lower. He may not be "up" to the entire battery of tests, but he could run a simple diagnostic on her.

He enjoyed the cute little landing strip of blond curls and her smoothly shaved folds below. The better to lick, and nibble, and…

When Kristen stiffened and cried out a while later, Luke suppressed a self-satisfied grin and crawled up beside her. With a sigh that turned into a moan, she nuzzled into his chest. "It's always the quiet ones…"

He didn't bother suppressing his grin this time and even chuckled as she kissed her way down to his navel. "I love how this thin line of hair—" she used one finger to trace the line as she spoke "—leads right to here." Her fingers burrowed down and then clasped around his cock. He closed his eyes and whispered her name.

"And...I may talk a lot, but I *can* do other things with my mouth." He lifted his head and opened his eyes in time to see his cock slide between her pretty lips. It was the most erotic thing he'd ever seen. Incredibly, he hardened. Physiologically improbable given the recovery time his body'd had. "Kristen."

She moaned in return and licked his length lovingly. Beginning with just the head, she sucked him into her mouth, then deeper, and deeper still. Instinctively, he held her head and raised his hips.

Lifting her mouth away, she moved one hand to cup his sack and the other to pump him. "Luke?"

"Yes, Kristen?" he groaned, and twitched as she licked the tip.

"Thank you for..." She closed her eyes and kissed down the length of him. "For being so..." Her voice wobbled.

"Hey." He sat up, quickly captured her in his arms and kissed away the tears on her cheeks. "You're beautiful."

She sniffed and gave him a shaky smile. "You're sweet."

"Sweet? Next you'll be calling me nice."

"And that's a bad thing?" She giggled.

"I'm not a hero, Kristen." He pressed her onto her back and came down on top of her. He kissed her deeply, gently biting her lower lip. She whimpered into his mouth as he fingered her thighs apart and entered her. Kristen's eyes flared with heat and her mouth turned up in approval. She seemed as turned-on by his show of dominance now as she had been by his tenderness before.

So, he let go.

Clenching his teeth, he unleashed a power behind his thrusts, where he'd held back before. She gasped and met his every move. He gripped her thigh and lifted her knee up beside her head and drove deep into her core. With a cry she bucked beneath him as he pumped faster. He felt her muscles tighten around him and barely managed to hold back a roar as he came long and hard.

Holding himself above her on one forearm, his breathing stuttered. She was still gulping in air as he slowly lowered himself to her side, his nose buried in her neck. A tender feeling swept over him, a wave of emotion so strong Luke forced himself to roll away from Kristen's soft body. As her hands slid from his back, she drew in a deep breath and let it out on a sigh.

He'd made a huge mistake.

Lying on his back, he ran his hands through his hair and rubbed his eyes with the heels of his hands. What the hell was he doing? He didn't know the exact statistics, but the chances of cancer recurring in a woman who'd had breast cancer so young... His throat tightened up. He couldn't lie here anymore. He had to get up. He didn't want to get involved with a woman like this. She'd just be one more person he couldn't save.

He eased away and she moaned, rolled over and curled up. Asleep. He watched her for a few seconds. God, she looked so young and vulnerable with her face relaxed in slumber. And yet she was a fighter. She had to be, after what she'd gone through. Some of the things she'd said to him came rushing back and made more sense now. About enjoying life, and daring to dream.

Climbing off the bed, he pulled the covers up and over her and then cleaned up in the bathroom, leaving the light on in case she woke up in the dark in a strange bed. Then he stalked out to the balcony to gulp in some much-needed fresh air.

He'd never get to sleep now. He paced the length of the balcony and realized he was rubbing his stomach. Maybe he needed to lay off the leftover Chinese.

Damn it. He'd felt so peaceful a mere half hour ago. And it wasn't just because it'd been a while since he'd had sex. There was something between them—him and Kristen. Something he might ordinarily have wanted to explore.

He stopped pacing to look out at the ocean. His fists clenched around the railing. It seemed as if death was mocking him. He'd flown halfway around the world to escape it, only to have a beautiful woman prod her way into his life. Make him feel something. Make him... care for her.

Before he let loose a primal yell, he pushed off the railing and went inside the condo. Could he convince himself this was just amazingly good sex influencing his thoughts? After all, he barely knew the girl. In another week or so she'd be on a plane back to California and he'd be back in Texas.

At his bedroom door, he stared at her, still curled up sweetly in his bed. The longing to climb in beside her and pull her into his arms and make love to her again was so strong he dug his nails into the door frame. If he did that, he might not be able to convince himself not to care for a girl whose life expectancy was about the same as a soldier's in Kabul right now.

Backing up slowly, he turned and strode to the recliner. He grabbed the remote, plopped down and clicked on the television. Nothing like late-night reruns to take one's mind off death, and women, and Chinese food gone bad.

8

KRISTEN WOKE UP SLOWLY, her dream, and the feelings it evoked, lingering as she rolled to her back. She'd dreamed she was diving, but without a mask or regulator or any other equipment. She was naked in warm, clear water. And Luke was naked, too, swimming with her, swirling around her and nudging her with his head like a male humpback courting a female.

She blinked and came fully awake, remembering where she was and what she'd done. A quick check of the king-size bed told her she was alone in it. The room was still dark, so it couldn't be morning yet. But the bathroom light was on.

Light flickered outside the hall doorway. The television? She slid out of bed, wrapping the comforter around her and dragging it with her as she peeked into the bathroom—empty—and then padded into the living room.

Luke was asleep in the recliner, wearing only a pair

of black boxer briefs. His head slanted at that angle was sure to give him a crick in his neck in the morning. His hands hung off the armrests and his right hand twitched. As Kristen moved closer his body jerked, and he mumbled something, but she couldn't make out the words.

Why was he out here? Could he not stand to sleep beside her in the bed? Had his tender acceptance of her scars only been an act? She couldn't believe he was that good an actor. Or maybe she wasn't that great a lover. She thought she'd felt something special between them as they made love. Geez. How naive was that?

Still, she'd rather have everything out in the open and know where she stood with him. Tentatively, she reached a hand toward him, and then drew it back. He'd told her he had trouble sleeping. She shouldn't wake him. But did that mean she should leave? Crawl back in his bed? Help herself to his shower? She'd never done this before and she wasn't sure about the protocol.

As she contemplated her situation, Luke grew increasingly agitated. He turned his head and his hand twitched again. Suddenly he jolted forward in the chair, gasping in air, his eyes wide-open, full of anguish.

Breathing harshly, he looked at her, but she could tell he didn't really see *her*. Then he blinked and he was back.

She closed the distance between them and touched his shoulder. "Luke?"

He glanced up and his expression drained of emotion. "Kristen." He tried to smile but it was a fairly dismal attempt. He reached for the remote and switched off the TV, throwing the room into darkness. The only light came from the bathroom down the hall.

"You had another nightmare."

Getting to his feet, he scrubbed a hand through his hair. "Yes."

Her throat felt tight as she tried to push words through it. "They must be really bad."

He shrugged. "Just another perk of the job."

She put her hands on his shoulders—which meant letting go of the comforter. "Don't do that. Talk to me."

His gaze dropped to her body, then darted away. "You're one to accuse me." Without facing her, he bent to retrieve the comforter, draped it around her and stalked to the bedroom.

Pain smacked her in the chest so hard her eyes watered. He couldn't stand to look at her body? Even in semidarkness? And what did he mean? What was she doing? She followed him into the bedroom. "What are you talking about?"

He was pulling on his jeans, but swung to face her, still unzipped. "I'm sure your doctor gave you the statistics. What are your chances, twenty-five percent? Thirty?" His words weren't thrown in anger, but more like tinged with anguish.

Still, Kristen flinched. He was talking about her chances for having a recurrence of cancer. "Something like that."

He glanced down to zip and button his jeans, and when he looked up, he wouldn't meet her gaze. "It's been a helluva night. Don't you have to be up early?"

His dismissive tone caused ice to seep into her bloodstream. "You're throwing me out? Just because my cancer might return someday? Why would that matter to you? You'll be long gone, halfway around the world."

"Exactly. What does any of it matter?"

She tried to swallow, but a lump had lodged itself in her throat. "Right. It doesn't. You scored some booty and now you're done. Whoo-hoo. Carve another notch in your bedpost, cowboy. Well, guess what? I got what I came for, too."

His jaw hitched and his eyes narrowed, but he didn't deny her words.

Flinging the comforter on the floor, she grabbed up her shirt and bra, her panties and grass skirt. He dropped his hands on his hips, turned his back and studied some spot on the wall.

He couldn't even look at her? Fine. She slammed into the bathroom and yanked her clothes on as fast as she could, muttering curse words as she dressed. She called him every bad name she could think of, wrapping herself in the protective cloak of indignation and anger.

When she stepped out he was sitting on the bed, still half-dressed, his expression unreadable. For once she had nothing to say. Couldn't have spoken if she had. Her chest felt as if she were a hundred feet under water.

She headed to the door, reached for the handle and turned it slowly, still hoping he might stop her from leaving, call her back, anything but the silence. After a moment, she looked down the hall. Then opened the door and left.

The anger calcified with every step to her own apartment until Kristen felt nothing. In this numb state, she texted Kekoa and canceled their diving for the day and showered in hot water until her skin was the color of a ripe tomato. Then she crawled between the sheets in her favorite old sweatshirt and curled up to ignore the world.

Gradually the numbness wore off and she started shivering. Luke was right. Her chances sucked. She'd been kidding herself. Fallen for the hype. She was probably going to die young. Why would any man take a chance on a future with someone who probably wouldn't be around?

And even if she beat it again, what man would want to have to nurse a bald, scarred woman? Luke sure as hell didn't.

She thought she'd been to the lowest, darkest place and come out the other side already, but this felt just as bad.

And what did she do the last time she'd felt like this? Ellen. Her support group back home. It always helped to talk to someone who'd been exactly where she was.

She snatched up her phone and almost hit Ellen's speed dial number. Wait. What time was it? 3:00 a.m. would be...6:00 a.m. back home. She couldn't call that early.

Putting the phone down, she lay back on the bed and imagined what Ellen would say. There are more and more survivors every year who live full lives. Attitude was the key. Kristen took a deep breath, inhaling positive energy and blowing out negative feelings. She didn't know if it really worked, but it sure as heck felt good. And proactive.

She was going to be a survivor for as long as she could. And she'd live a fulfilling and happy life with or without a man. Most of the women in her support group were married. Of course, most of those women had husbands who loved them *before* they got cancer.

And some had divorced, too.

Some spouses just couldn't hack it.

But Luke was a doctor. Not that he was anywhere near being a spouse, but somehow, subconsciously or not, his being a doctor had made her feel more comfortable exposing herself to him.

In her gut, she knew he wasn't the type of guy who kept score of his conquests with notches on a bedpost. If he was, he'd have never agreed to just being friends. He'd have dropped her and had some other woman lined up the minute she bailed on the lovemaking the first time. Heck, he'd turned her down for dinner when they initially met. The exact opposite of a player. And he'd been so sweet once he'd discovered her scars.

A sob broke and Kristen buried her face in a pillow.

No, she'd understood his problem correctly the first time. It'd just been easier to leave him while feeling a dose of righteous anger. But he'd said it himself. Her chances of cancer returning were high. And he couldn't deal with that. So, before they got any closer, he was backing out.

She couldn't blame him. She'd learned to live with the very real possibility of recurrence two years ago. But it wasn't fair to expect him to.

He couldn't even deal with the deaths in his hospital in Afghanistan. What had he said that day he took the sleeping pills? He couldn't save them. As if he expected to never lose a patient. He wasn't a superhero who could save the world.

But even a superhero could be haunted by the violent deaths of so many soldiers.

AMY SAT INSIDE THE COFFEE shop a couple of blocks from Tradewinds, swinging her crossed leg while she waited for Kekoa to show up. She checked the time on her cell phone again and then scanned the sidewalk outside. Her shift started in an hour. How had Kekoa even gotten her cell-phone number to ask her to meet him here?

She heard him before she saw him. The deep rumbling of his motorcycle stopped and Kekoa set the kickstand down, swung his leg over the seat and took off his helmet.

The door to the coffee shop opened and he walked in, moving with the lithe grace of a panther. His dark, penetrating gaze landed on her in the crowd and his nostrils flared as if he'd spotted his prey. He wore a tight-fitting black T-shirt that only made his dark native skin look darker. It hugged every contour of every muscle in his chest and abdomen. And his biceps? How was it legal to be packing those kinds of guns without a permit?

Okay, cool it with the mental drooling, girl. He's just a man.

He sat at her table without taking his eyes off her. Why was she drinking a hot cappuccino when the room was already so hot? And crowded. Too many customers were sucking all the oxygen from the shop. She grabbed a napkin, patted the back of her neck and tried to catch a breath.

"Thank you for agreeing to meet me." His tone sounded polite, humble even. But his posture was tense, as if he were ready to pounce if she dared try to escape.

She wasn't sure she'd mind being captured.

What kind of crazy thought was that? She was an independent woman, answerable to no one but herself. "I did it for Kris."

Liar.

His beautiful lips flattened. "I realize the last time we talked I made some assumptions. And I insulted you. I apologize."

She raised her brows, keeping her expression bland, even though her heart was racing. "Okay."

His fists clenched on the table and so did his jaw.

The dimples, which she'd fallen head over heels for the first time she saw him, appeared.

Amy had taken one look at Kekoa and nearly turned both ankles. *Beautiful* was too lame a word for the man. His short-cropped black hair set off the smooth mahogany skin of his jaw. And there probably wasn't one ounce of fat on the man.

"Okay? That's all you have to say?"

"I—I don't know what else to say."

He leaned forward and took her hand across the table. "Don't play games with me. I still desire you. I think only of you. Do you feel the same?"

Ice water. She needed a glass of ice water. So she could dump it over her head. She pulled her hand away from his and drew in a ragged breath. "It's not that simple."

"Why not?"

"You said it was your duty to—how did you put it?— 'make an alliance' with someone appropriate. How has that changed?"

He frowned. "It hasn't."

"So, I'd be your girlfriend on the side?"

He straightened. "No! I wouldn't dishonor my wife so. But we aren't even engaged yet. And I want you now—"

"Hold on." She lifted her hand palm up. "What do you mean, you aren't engaged *yet*? So you already have someone lined up to be Mrs. Kekoa?"

"Well." He sat back. "As I said. Nothing has been decided officially."

Good grief, he was unofficially engaged? "Look. I know I was…willing before. More than willing. But that was before I realized how inappropriate I am for you."

His eyes flared. "I have apologized for—"

"Let me finish. The truth is, I wouldn't mind…continuing what we started."

He grinned and his dimples broke out in full force. It was almost her undoing. "I knew—"

"And it's not that I want any kind of commitment from you, God forbid."

"Why do you say it like that?" He scowled. "God forbid I was committed to you? Why is that a bad thing?"

"It's just an expression. It means I don't want to be married ever again."

His eyes widened and he tucked in his chin. "You were married?"

She raised her brows. "Is that so hard to believe?"

"That's not what I meant. But, you don't wish to be married again, then what's to stop us from being together now?"

Amy sighed, long and loud. "It's just that…" Nothing but brutal honesty would do at this moment. "No matter how attracted I am, I won't be with someone who considers me below them." She mumbled under her breath, "Not again."

"What?"

"I guess what I'm saying is…" She scooted back her chair and got to her feet. When he also stood she looked him in the eye. "I don't forgive you." She wound her way around tables and chairs and marched out the door.

AS UNPLEASANT AS HER CHAT with Kekoa had been, Amy got the feeling Kristen's night with Luke had been disastrous.

The fact that Kristen looked as if she'd spent the day pouring lemon juice in her eyes was the first clue. The second was that Kristen wouldn't talk about it. Not even on their break. As Amy waited for an order of drinks at the bar, Kristen walked up with an order for the bartender.

Amy gave her a pointed glare. "I guess I'm going to have to feed Captain Mysterious's man parts to the sharks, after all."

Not only did Kristen not smile, but she actually flinched and squeezed her eyes closed.

"Oh, no. Kris, I'm so sorry." She put an arm around her friend. "I thought a little joke would cheer you up. Are you going to be all right?"

Kristen swiped at her cheeks and nodded. She lifted a quivering chin and took a deep breath. "What about your meeting with Kekoa? What did he have to say?"

Collecting her cocktails from the bartender and setting them quickly on her tray, Amy shrugged. "He asked me out again, I turned him down again."

"Did he insult you again?" Kristen stacked her customers' drinks on a tray.

"No, he apologized." Amy spun and headed slowly toward her section.

Kristen followed. "He did? Then why—"

Amy stopped and faced her friend. "He has a fiancée."

Halted in her tracks, Kristen stared with her mouth hung open. Then her eyes narrowed and her mouth tightened. "Men." She headed off to her section and Amy left for hers.

A few seconds later, Amy heard a loud crash of breaking glass. She looked up in time to see Kristen with her hands over her mouth and one of her customers standing, wiping liquid off his pants. Kristen seemed frozen at first, but then raced to the bathroom. Amy grabbed a couple of towels and headed to Kristen's table to help clean up, and Frank appeared to mollify the gentleman and offer free drinks for the table.

As soon as she'd dropped the drink order off at the bar, Amy darted into the bathroom.

Kristen was sitting on the counter, red-eyed and sniffling. "Frank stuck his head in the door and told me to go home," she said with a stuffed-up nose.

"Oh, hon." Amy gave her a hug. "You probably should've just called in sick."

"I didn't want to leave you shorthanded."

"We'll be fine." She hoisted herself onto the counter beside Kristen. "So much for your wild island fling, huh?" She nudged her shoulder.

Kristen snorted. "Yeah."

"Well, you still have another week. I say you go out there, find a hottie with a body, take him back to your place and—"

"Yeah, 'cause that worked so well for you." Kristen managed to look disapproving even while wiping her nose with a handful of tissue.

Amy chuckled and draped her arm around her friend. "Well, if I can't feed his man parts to the sharks, then what can I do to help?"

Kristen giggled and shook her head. "Nothing. You can't blame the guy. He has a perfectly legitimate fear. I could get cancer again anytime, and it's not fair to ask anyone to go through that with me."

Amy's heart squeezed at the thought of Kristen getting sick again. She was such a strong person. To go through what she'd gone through... "Is that what he said?"

"No. Um, not exactly. But it doesn't matter. I'll be fine." Then she straightened her spine, drew back her shoulders and lifted her chin. "As a matter of fact, I'm going to be more than fine. I decided the day I got the all clear from the doc that I wasn't going to live the rest of my life in fear. I was going to spend each day celebrating life and living it to the fullest."

"Good for you!" Amy cheered for her friend, but Kristen's words socked her in the gut. Hadn't she decided something similar when she'd escaped her abusive ex? No more living her life in fear. She'd wanted a fresh start, a new life. And she'd made one for herself here. But now, it seemed she was letting old fears prevent her from doing what she really wanted.

So what if Kekoa got married in a few weeks or months? He was single now. And what they'd had together, well, she knew enough to know that kind of sizzle didn't come along every day.

And if she were really honest with herself, she had to admit she was afraid of that passion. She lost herself when she was that attracted to someone. And Kekoa was just the kind of dominant male she was obviously attracted to. He'd swallow her up and spit her back out when he was done with her. But he could only take whatever she was willing to give over to him.

Could she have a passionate affair and not lose herself in the process?

She gave a mental shrug and returned her focus to Kristen. "So, shall we go do something wild and crazy tomorrow? Forget about Kekoa and the Captain and do something girly?"

Kristen was eyeing her speculatively, the light finally coming back to shine in her baby blues. "Not sure about girly, but…how about something *gnarly?*"

9

KRISTEN DRAGGED HER NEWLY rented surfboard down the sloping sand to the spot on the beach where Amy had chosen to set up her chair and umbrella. "Are you sure you don't mind me leaving you alone for a bit?" She couldn't wait to feel the thrill of riding the waves. If she were going to leave fear behind and forget about her vacation-fling-gone-bad, this was the way to do it.

"Are you kidding? You think I want the competition of you tanning next to me?" She grinned and plunked a huge hat on her head.

No way could Kristen compete with Amy's long legs and big boobs. Especially not in that hot-pink bikini. Of course, Kristen would have to actually wear a bikini....

One fear at a time. For now her wet suit would be better protection for surfing anyway.

She and Amy had taken the day off from work and driven north along the coast forty-five minutes to La-haina. Kristen had painted her toenails on the dashboard of Amy's old Toyota as they'd sung along to old favorites. Later they were planning on checking out the bars around the beach resorts for lunch and Margaritas, and then they were signed up for hula-dancing lessons. All things Kristen had wanted to do before she had to go home.

It wasn't even noon and Amy had slathered on sunscreen in addition to bringing the umbrella.

"Don't you want to get any sun at all?"

Amy tugged her sunglasses down her nose and glared at Kristen over the rims. "You've obviously never seen what happens when a redhead tries to tan. Trust me, it's not pretty."

Kristen giggled. It felt good to laugh again.

"Now shoo." Amy waved her away. "You're blocking my view." She turned a brilliant smile toward three young muscled guys walking past. They ogled. She ogled. It was fun to watch. For about half a second. The waves were calling to Kristen stronger than any men ogling.

There was a coral reef at Napili Bay that kept waves from getting too big and since she wasn't as experienced at surfing that suited her fine. The wave report at the rental shop had announced a storm brewing that might hit shore later in the afternoon and bring a few ten-footers with it. She'd be done by then.

As soon as she'd paddled out past the breakers, she heard a very distant rumble of thunder, but she barely registered it as she saw an excellent wave heading her way. She jumped to her feet to catch the curl, but crashed about halfway in. She controlled the fall once she realized she'd lost her balance, and found her board thankfully still attached by the Velcro anklet.

A half hour later she'd caught three more decent waves. One she'd been able to ride all the way to shore, which earned her high fives from several of the other surfers. Man, that felt great!

But she still hadn't caught a really big one. And the waves were getting higher. The sky was also getting darker. Probably best to make this her last ride.

She waved to Amy, who casually waved back while busy flirting with a couple of older gentlemen in a golf cart with the Napili Bay Resort logo on the back. Then Kristen paddled far out to where the large waves were breaking. She sat up, straddling her board, and paddled around, dodging some nice but not quite right waves, waiting for the perfect ride.

While she waited, it started spitting rain, just a sprinkle here and there, but it made her look up and what she saw worried her. Thick, dark clouds hung low right above the surf. A loud crack of thunder boomed so close it made her jump. She scanned the shore and saw Amy, a tiny figure in the distance waving frantically for her to come in. A lifeguard stood next to her, also motioning her in.

Waves were huge now and rolling in right on top of each other. Well, if she was going to catch a massive one, it was now or never. Oh, geez! The mother of all waves was coming right at her. She paddled hard to position herself, jumped to her feet and rode the break for what seemed like minutes, but was probably only seconds when the wave seemed to swell like a monster opening its mouth.

The current sucked her under and she flipped off, head over heels into the cold, salty water. The undertow sucked her out and kept her under. Her only hope was the board still attached to her ankle.

She swam up, and up some more, struggling just to reach the surface before she ran out of air. Finally, she broke through the choppy water and gasped in air. As she searched for her board, the rough waves slammed into her and her head exploded in pain.

THE DOG WHINED AGAIN and stuck his cold, wet nose under Luke's hand, nudging him to get his attention. It was almost noon. He'd been up most of the night, and taken the dog with him on his 6:00 a.m. run.

"All right, you needy, flea-bitten, walking hulk of shedding hair." Luke pushed himself out of the recliner and stalked to the bedroom for a shirt.

The dog went haywire the second Luke got up, barking, racing back and forth between the bedroom and front door.

"Yeah, yeah, I'm coming." Yanking a shirt over his head and shoving it down over his stomach, Luke grabbed the leash off the table by the front door and hooked it onto the dog's collar. He reached into his jeans pocket, pulled out a dog treat and fed it to the tan mutt. Hunkering down, he rubbed him behind his black ears and patted his back. "You know I'd keep you if I could, don't you?"

He rubbed the dog's sides and down his back a little more and then straightened, wondering where that sentiment had come from. He couldn't care for a dog any better than he could a girlfriend with cancer.

As he'd been doing for the past two days, he forced himself to be realistic, to be practical. He couldn't bring a dog from Hawaii to the mainland, and he couldn't keep seeing a girl who needed a guy who could be there for her through thick and thin. Kristen would only be dragged down by someone like him. After what he'd done to her the other night? Yeah, he was a real catch.

He took the dog for a long walk, thinking how he'd miss the dumb animal. Not only was the mutt company, but he'd forced Luke to get outside into fresh air, like a certain petite blonde had. He realized he thought about things while he walked the dog. Whether that was a good thing or not...

Because, mostly, he thought about Kristen. And if she was okay after things had gone to hell the night before last. She was better off without him, for sure. Any good he might have done by helping her see that her scars were nothing compared to the beauty she radiated just by smiling, was obliterated by how he'd handled the rest of the night.

What an ass he'd been. How could he have done that to her?

Damn it, didn't he have other things he could think about? He'd gotten emails from his mom and one sister. Mom had finally gotten a hearing aid. His nephew was starting Little League in a couple of weeks, and wanted to use Luke's old mitt. Hard to believe his younger sisters already had kids in grade school.

He used to want kids. Now? He wasn't so sure.

He stopped in his tracks, the dog yanking on the leash. When had he changed so much? Sure, he was going through a rough period, but...

The dog yanked again and Luke turned to head toward the condo. Confiscating an empty box from behind the Quick-Mart, he led the dog back to the condo, made sure he drank plenty of water and then packed up the dog bowls and food, and all the other dog paraphernalia he'd acquired over the past couple of weeks.

The mutt's scrapes had all healed. The vet had given him the basic shots he needed. It was time to find someone else to take care of him.

Luke clipped the leash back on the dog and led him out to the rented Jeep.

The directions to the animal shelter were on a sticky note attached to the bag of the dog's favorite treats. He dug the bag out of the box of dog stuff, gave the dog another treat and set out for the shelter. As he drove, it seemed as if he could feel the dog's eyes on him. He glanced over at a light and sure enough, the mutt was staring at him.

"Aw, now, don't look at me like that. This is for your own good."

The dog whined and turned his back to Luke, curling up in the seat.

Damn it.

He pulled up outside the shelter and got the dog out. Luke's chest tightened. And once he got inside and heard the barks and whines of the other animals in the shelter, he looked down at the mutt, his tongue lolling out the side of his mouth, gazing up at him with such trust. Then he looked back up to the busy girl standing behind the counter waiting for him to fill out the paperwork.

He couldn't do it. How did he know the dog would get adopted? Cute puppies always went first. Then purebreds. But a mutt like his dog? No. He'd have to find someone he knew would really care for the mutt.

Twenty minutes later he was back at the condo, throwing his keys on the table and unpacking the dog's bowls.

He needed to find a good home for the mutt. The only people he knew who lived on the island were Kristen's boat driver and her friend, Amy. Maybe one of them would know someone. But in order to talk to them he'd have to call Kristen. Or he could drop by Tradewinds when Amy was there.

Where the waitstaff or regular patrons might recognize him from that night he'd resuscitated the old man. He didn't want that kind of attention.

It was the lesser of two evils then. The longer he put off getting rid of the dog, the harder it would be to give him up. And wasn't it ironic that he felt the same way about Kristen?

But when he dialed her cell, it wasn't her voice that answered.

"Luke?" It was a high shaky female voice that sounded as if she'd been crying. Why was Amy answering Kristen's phone?

Luke's stomach squeezed. "What's wrong? Where's Kristen?"

He heard a sniff and the sound of the phone being muffled with voices in the background. "She can't come to the phone right now, can I take a message?"

Was she kidding? "Listen, Amy. Let me talk to her."

"I told you she can't talk, you cretin."

He heard the phone shuffle around again, but this time he heard something that sent dread racing through his veins. He'd recognize the sound of a doctor being called over a hospital speaker system anywhere.

Oh, God. "Amy. Is she…" He closed his eyes and prayed like he hadn't prayed since he'd had the faith of a child. "Is she going to be okay?"

"I'm hanging up now."

"Please! Amy? Amy! I'll call every hospital on Maui if I have to."

He heard another sniff. "And then what?"

"And then I can be there for her."

"I thought you didn't want to be there for her."

Luke gritted his teeth, stifling all the names he wanted to call himself. "I was wrong, Amy. So wrong."

She sighed, a second went by, then another. "West Maui Memorial, in Lahaina."

The phone went dead, but he still didn't know what was wrong. If Kristen was going to be okay, or not. And in the end, he supposed it didn't matter. He was going.

Knocking on every door on his floor until he found some wonderful soul to promise to look in on his dog and walk him until he got back, Luke left the woman his key, threw a change of clothes and all his extra cash in a duffel. Once in the Jeep, he programmed the GPS for the hospital and set out for Lahaina.

KRISTEN HEARD SOMEONE calling her name. It sounded like Luke, but different. This voice full of emotion, and huskier, as if he hadn't had anything to drink in a long time.

"Kristen, please, wake up so I can tell you how sorry I am." She felt him squeeze her hand, and then she felt his warm lips on the back of it. "God, Kristen, please. Please, wake up."

She wanted to tell him she would eventually, but she just needed to sleep a bit longer. She tried to open her mouth but when she did, no sound came out. She was dreaming. Luke wouldn't be here. There was something wrong.

But it felt so right when he rubbed her arm. And she recognized his scent as he got closer and pressed a kiss to her forehead. She wanted to call him back when she sensed him move away. But he soon took her hand again. And this time he didn't let go.

"Kristen."

Someone was calling her name again. A woman this time. Had the time before been just a dream? She thought she answered, but the woman called her name again. They wouldn't stop bugging her. Asking her to open her eyes and tell them her name. Didn't they know her name already since they were calling her by it?

If she opened her eyes and spoke it wouldn't feel as nice as it felt here in this dark, peaceful place.

"Kristen!"

"What?" She opened her eyes to glare at the pest who wouldn't leave her alone. But she immediately closed them again, grimacing and moaning at the agonizing pain in her head. Some little devils were having a good time driving sharp needles into her temples.

"Kristen?" The woman's voice was softer this time. Kinder.

"Yes?" There. See? She answered.

"I've given you some more medicine for the pain. Can you open your eyes a little longer this time?"

Oh, all right. They weren't going to leave her in peace until she complied. She grudgingly, gingerly opened her eyes and blinked at the blurry figure. She was a tall, dark-skinned woman, probably mid-fifties, and she was smiling.

"That's very good. I'm Doctor Ōpūnui. Now, I have the room darkened, but I need to check your dilation, so I'm going to have to shine a bright light into each eye, but I'll try to go as quickly as possible. Ready?"

Kristen tried to nod, but it hurt. The eye check followed, and then some blessed soul held a straw to her lips and the water tasted heavenly to her parched mouth. All she could see for a moment was the light flashing in her eyes.

But even once her eyes adjusted to the dark again, her vision was still blurry. Wait. Why was she in the hospital again? Hadn't she finished all her treatments and surgeries?

She looked around the room and saw a fuzzy, tall, redheaded woman step out of the shadows.

"Kris?" The woman moved closer. "Do you know who I am?"

As if someone had switched on a movie projector and played a montage of her life in Hawaii in fast-forward, memories came flooding back. "Amy!" She smiled and Amy smiled back. And then she started crying.

"Oh, damn." Amy turned and grabbed a box of tissues.

"Geez, do I look that bad?"

Amy gasped as she shifted back to face Kristen. "No! I'm just so glad to see you awake."

Hmm, that didn't sound good. How long had she been asleep? Had she missed the deadline for the *Geographic Universe* contest? "How long was I out?" *Please don't let the deadline have passed.*

"You've been unconscious for thirty-one hours." The doctor stepped into her line of vision. "Do you remember what happened?"

She let out a relieved breath. Hours. Not days. Not months. What had happened? "I was…surfing."

"Thankfully there was a lifeguard from the resort down there talking to Amy," a deep voice mumbled somewhere in the shadows behind Amy.

"Luke?" She tried to lift her head, but it hurt and she winced.

A tall, dark form stepped out of the shadows. "Kristen."

He said her name in that same raspy voice she'd heard in her…dream. "What are you doing here?" She switched her gaze to Amy. "Did you call him?"

The doctor cleared her throat. "I'll send a nurse in to check your wound and change your bandages." She addressed Amy. "I'll give you five minutes each and then our patient needs to rest." With a last nod to Kristen, she hustled out the door.

Amy took her hand and a memory of Luke holding her hand while she slept popped into her head. But that couldn't be a memory if she'd been asleep. It must've been a dream.

"Luke called your cell a few hours after…the accident. And he insisted on coming and he hasn't left your side—despite my protests—since." She glared at Luke, and then softened her expression when she looked back at Kristen. "Oh, Kris. I'm so glad you woke up." Tears filled Amy's eyes, but she suddenly looked angry. "Don't ever scare me like that again!"

"I won't. I'm so sorry, Amy." Kristen's eyes stung.

"Better not." Amy's glare changed to a smile and she bent down and hugged Kristen gently, then stepped back.

Luke stepped close to her bed. His face was unreadable, but his eyes were bloodshot and his jaw had several days of stubble. He took her hand, but it was really her wrist. He placed two fingers over her artery and brought his left arm up to look at his wristwatch. He was taking her pulse?

Although... His touch may have tried to be impersonal, but his hand trembled. Still, she preferred the passionate man from last night. The man calling her name, begging her to wake up. "Am I gonna live, Doc?"

He let go and folded his arms across his chest. "You were lucky. The CT showed no signs of intracranial hemorrhaging."

"In English, please?"

Unfolding his arms, he nodded toward the heart monitor beside the bed. "A blow to the head like you sustained could've resulted in brain damage, coma or..." His lips flattened and he clenched his jaw. His eyes watered. "You could've died, Kristen. I—we—I could've lost you." He grabbed her hand, the whole hand, and squeezed it between both of his.

Great. Now her eyes were watering, too. But there, at last, was the emotion she'd wanted to feel from him.

Her head still hurt, as though it was being struck by a miniature pickax. "I needed to feel alive. I've told you. I know what my chances are, okay? And I won't let fear stop me from living every minute to the fullest." Her stomach roiled and she laid her head back against the pillow.

"What is it?" Luke let go of her hand and felt her forehead.

"I wasn't reckless. I checked the weather report. The storm just blew in early." She moaned, feeling violently sick.

"Kristen?" He moved his fingertips to just under her ears, feeling along her jawline.

She moaned again, rolled to her side and threw up all over him.

10

KRISTEN AWOKE WITH A DULL ache behind her right ear. And a hot, heavy weight across her hips.

She slowly opened her eyes. The faint light of early morning struggled through the hospital blinds. Luke was asleep with his arm across her hips and his head lying on the bed beside her. His stubble was even thicker this morning, and she detected lines around his eyes and mouth even with his face relaxed in sleep. Oh, how she wanted to run her hand over his dark, tousled hair. And kiss those masculine lips.

But he'd hurt her to the core the other day. And they were just supposed to be having a fun holiday fling.

Oh, God. She'd puked on him last night. Embarrassment swamped over her again. And he'd been so sweet about it. Making sure the nurse came in to help her before leaving to clean himself up.

She didn't remember much after the nurse came in. Kristen's head had pounded with pain and by the time her bandage was changed she was exhausted and must've fallen back to sleep.

Somehow Luke had managed to find a way to shower and borrow some scrubs, and…he'd spent the night next to her. Again. Amy said he hadn't left her side. Did that mean he'd changed his mind about her? But, this was just a bump on the head. Not cancer.

Where was Amy? Kristen glanced over at the empty recliner in the corner. When she looked back at Luke, his deep brown eyes were lazily open and staring at her. This close, she could see the coffee-colored irises had thin bands of gold around the edges.

"Hi." That one breathy word was all the vocabulary she could manage with his gaze locked onto hers.

"Hi," he answered. Then he blinked and raised his head, scowling. He straightened and ran a hand down his jaw, looking adorably perplexed.

He got to his feet, ran both hands through his hair and then glanced at her again. "How are you feeling?" He pulled the chair away from the bed.

She must've felt better because the only thing she could think about was how sexy he looked.

Look away. Think of something else!

"Better than last night." She winced. "Sorry about that."

"Perfectly normal symptom of a concussion." He gave her a warm smile that was gone too soon. Turning all doctory, he checked her bandage, her IV, her blood-pressure readouts, her heart rate. He certainly looked like a doctor in those scrubs. All that was missing was a white coat and a stethoscope around his neck.

And he had a nice bedside manner... *Don't go there.*

"Luke?"

"Hmm?" He turned his attention back to her. "How is the pain? Should I get them to increase your meds?"

"Maybe, a little." She lifted her hand to the bandage behind her right ear.

His expression changed from professional detachment to furrowed brows and worry. "I'll go get a nurse." He came back with a nurse who fiddled with her IV, told her the doctor and her breakfast would be by in a little bit.

Once the nurse left, Luke glanced at the closed door, then dragged the chair back to the bed and sat, taking her hand in his.

Kristen sighed, savoring the heat of his hand in her cold one.

"Look, I'm sorry. For the other day."

"It's—" not *all right,* her usual answer "—understandable."

He grimaced. "I wouldn't have blamed you if you'd kicked me out of your room last night."

"Well, I tried throwing up on you, but you just came back." She grinned mischievously.

He huffed a laugh. "Wasn't the first time that's happened to me." His smile faded. "Or the worst thing I've been covered in."

She assumed he meant blood, and she didn't want

to know if he meant something else. "You mentioned Kabul once. Is that where you're stationed?"

He frowned, studying her hand where he'd entwined his fingers with hers. "The National Military Hospital there."

"I've heard of Kabul from the news. Lots of suicide bombers. One even infiltrated your hospital, didn't he?"

He winced and his jaw clenched and then shifted to the left. "Let's talk about something—"

"What made you want to become a doctor?"

His frown intensified. He rubbed the stubble on his chin. "My father."

"He was a doctor, too?"

Luke shook his head, his mouth half curved. "A truck driver." His grip on her fingers tightened. "He just got up from the dinner table one night and dropped to the floor. While my mom called 9-1-1, I rolled him over and tried to remember the CPR class we took in Boy Scouts when I was younger."

"Geez. How old were you?"

"Twelve."

Kristen gasped. "That's so young."

He shrugged. "Old enough to have known CPR. If I had…"

"I'm sorry."

Staring at their joined hands, he nodded. "Last person I told about that was my Army ROTC recruiter."

"I'm sure you already know this…" She hesitated,

but decided to just say it. "Even if you'd done every-thing perfectly, it might not have saved him."

He drew in a deep breath and let it out again. "I know." He raised his dark gaze to hers. "I know I don't deserve it, but I'd like a second chance. After you get out of here, I want to see you until I have to leave. If you're feeling up to it."

Her heart jumped and she almost said yes. But she wasn't sure it'd be a good idea to spend any more time with him at this point. He'd made his position clear. And her feelings...well, they were more than they should be for a fun holiday fling.

"You don't have to answer right now." He squeezed her hand reassuringly.

Kristen kept her eyes closed, savoring the feel of his hand and the crisp, clean scent that was pure Luke.

His hand went to her forehead and he frowned.

"What?"

"You feel a little warm." He got to his feet, scooting the chair back. "I'm going to get a nurse to take your temperature."

"Wait." Kristen was pretty sure her fevered brow wasn't from an actual fever. "What are you doing here, Luke?"

He stiffened his stance and his expression turned all detached again. "Your doctor said you needed to be monitored closely over the next twenty-four hours."

"So, you're my own personal monitor? If this is be-cause you feel guilty about the other night...?"

"Guilt has nothing to do with it."

"Then why—"

"Because I care about you. All right? I couldn't think straight when I thought you might..." His lips tightened, but his eyes still burned into her.

"If I had died out there, it wouldn't have been your fault, Luke."

"I know that."

She looked away. "I don't think you do."

"Well, you'll just have to endure my presence until you're discharged. Amy got called in to work last night right after you fell asleep. I promised to take care of you and bring you home if you were released."

"Oh." Her stomach growled and Luke left to track down her breakfast. At least, that was his excuse.

Kristen closed her eyes, her mind tumbling from one thought to the next. A part of her couldn't believe Luke was here, and the way he was acting... So different. More open. Telling her about his father, for instance. Was it guilt, as she suspected? Or maybe it was the hospital setting. He *did* seem at home here, more confident, not so shy.

She realized he was in his element here. Helping people. Saving lives. That's what he'd set out to do after his father died. But it was a mission doomed to fail. He couldn't save everyone. That's what he'd said that day he took the sleeping pills. And that's what was eating him up inside.

Somehow, she wished she could make him see that

even heroes were human, with human limitations. And he needed to accept and forgive that part of himself.

The door opened and a nurse rolled in a computer, ready to take her vitals. A volunteer followed her in with a tray of breakfast. There was a knock and when Kristen called, "Come in," Luke stuck his head around the edge of the door.

"Doing all right?"

"Luke." He'd only left fifteen minutes ago, and yet she missed him as if he'd been gone for days. "I want to go home. I mean, back to the condo." Why was she on the verge of tears?

"I'm on it." His head disappeared.

And, true to his word, by lunchtime, she'd signed her discharge papers and was being wheeled out to Luke's Jeep.

LUKE NOTICED KRISTEN'S eyes closing several times on the forty-five-minute drive home, and by the time he pulled the Jeep into a parking space at the condominium, she was asleep.

He picked her up and carried her to her condo, surprised at how little she weighed. She was petite, but well toned, her arm and leg muscles defined. She moaned and snuggled into his chest. Even when he set her down to unlock her door, she kept her arms around him and her cheek against him. Tucking her into bed was no hardship either. He got her out of her shorts, but left her shirt and panties on, then pulled the thick coverlet up to her neck.

Promising to be back in an hour to check on her, he left to get his dog from his neighbor, took the mutt out for a run and then showered himself. There'd been no conversation between him and Kristen since breakfast, which suited him fine. He didn't know what had possessed him to talk about himself so much this morning.

He'd been so damned grateful she was alive, he'd have done anything, told her anything she wanted to know. He'd been an ass and he'd been given a second chance to make up for it.

As he was leaving for Kristen's, the mutt whined and gave him that accusing look. Luke couldn't abandon him again. "All right. Come on."

He felt as if he wore the same dopey grin his dog did as he rode down the elevator. He was anxious to get back to Kristen. He'd get her something to eat. Check her bandage, her pupil dilation and her blood pressure. And, though it was too soon for sex, he'd like to hold her while she slept. Just to have her in his arms.

As he let himself in with Kristen's key, his heart was racing, he could hear voices. Had something hap...

He stopped short a couple steps in.

"Luke," Amy called to him from the kitchen. "I wondered if you'd taken Kris's key." She was scooping something from a saucepan into a bowl.

Kristen's boat driver, Kekoa, sat at the bar, glaring at him. "She had to get up to let us in."

Luke blinked. His first thought was, *Then why didn't you stay home?* His second was more charitable. These people were her friends. She must have called them. Wanted them here.

"How is she?" The dog growled at Kekoa and Kekoa stood glaring down at the canine, challenging him. The dog barked.

"Oh, Kris told me you'd adopted a dog." Amy came out of the kitchen and put herself between the dog and Kekoa. She squatted and extended her hand palm up and Dog sniffed at it before licking it. "That's a good boy. What a good boy!" Amy rubbed the dog's head and under his neck and back.

"I was going to take him to the shelter nearby, but I thought I'd see if you knew anyone who wanted him first." Luke cleared his throat. That was mostly the truth.

"Oh, I'll take him!" Amy's eyes lit up as she looked at Luke. "I'd feel so much safer in my place with a dog around."

He didn't look much like a watchdog right now, rolled over, presenting Amy his tummy to rub, and his tongue lolled out to the side.

"You don't feel safe in your apartment?" Kekoa scowled.

Amy stilled, then straightened and faced Kekoa with a brilliant smile. "I will now." She sashayed back into the kitchen and came out carrying a tray with a bowl, spoon, mug and napkin on it.

"I'll take that to her." Luke stepped up, hands extended to take the tray.

"Oh, that's okay." Amy smiled but ignored his hands and continued down the hallway.

Luke hesitated. He didn't feel he could just walk into her bedroom now. Uninvited. Barging in on her privacy.

"You planned to check her blood pressure?" Kekoa appeared beside him, nodding toward the BP cuff and stethoscope Luke had dug out of his luggage and brought with him.

"Yes. As well as her pupils and the cut on her head."

"Sounds like a good idea." Kekoa nodded. "Go on in, but we probably shouldn't keep her too long from resting."

Luke bristled at the order. "I think I can restrain myself." He raised a brow and stared down the arrogant boat driver.

Kekoa's eyes narrowed. "She's a good friend. I don't like seeing her hurt."

The inference being that Luke would do something to hurt Kristen. But, of course, he had, hadn't he? Still, he ground his teeth in frustration. "Does Amy have to work this evening?"

"Yes. But you don't need to worry. I'll be staying."

Like hell. "If anyone is going to stay with Kristen tonight, it'll be me." He leaned in, displaying the time-honored nonverbal communication of dominance.

"She doesn't need you around right now." Kekoa leaned in, too, and practically growled.

"I'm a doctor, don't tell me what she needs." Luke gritted his teeth.

"What is going on?" Amy appeared in the hallway, fists on hips.

"As a medical professional, I'm the best qualified—"

But Kekoa was speaking at the same time. "This *haole* thinks he can just barge in here—"

"What did you just call me?"

"I'm staying with Kristen tonight and that's final," Kekoa ground out between his teeth.

"Like hell you are."

"Hey!" Amy shouted to get their attention. "Neither one of you are staying. Kristen wants you both to go home. Luke?" She walked over to him. "You can go in now, but when she starts acting sleepy, it's time for you to go."

Damn it. He couldn't remember the last time he'd felt like a schoolboy getting a lecture from the principal. Chastised, Luke unclenched his fists, schooled his features and nodded.

"Kekoa." She turned to face the boat driver. "Thank you for coming, but there's no reason for you to stay."

Kekoa's scowl grew more menacing and he raised a hand to run through his hair. As he did, Amy flinched away, her arm raised in front of her face as if to protect herself from a blow.

Luke blinked.

Amy dropped her arms to her sides and lifted her chin.

Kekoa stepped close to Amy, took her by the shoulders. "Amy. You think I'd hit you?" She shrugged and glanced away. He bent and whispered in her ear.

"No. Kekoa, please, go."

Luke couldn't have resisted that pleading tone either and Kekoa stalked out the door.

Without another word, Amy stepped aside, gesturing for Luke to go into the bedroom.

The way Kristen smiled when she saw him was like balm to his wounded ego. "Hey."

He didn't have to work up the smile he gave her, even if her pallor was slightly worrisome. She was sitting up and eating, and she looked so damned beautiful, he wanted to gather her up into his arms and kiss every inch of her.

He took her hand the second he sat on the bed beside her. "I had to leave to go check on—"

"This big ol' mutt?" The dog had followed Amy back and made himself at home on the end of Kristen's bed. "Of course you did." She bit her bottom lip and held tight to his hand. "Thought you were going to take him to a shelter." Brows raised, she gave him a skeptical smile.

He shrugged. "The dog didn't want to go."

Her smile widened into a full-out grin. "He seems well behaved. Amy says she's going to adopt him from you? That sure works out well. I think Amy needs a pet. And if that's the case, we need to name him. Amy and I were just suggesting names. What do you think of Max? Or Blackbeard? Since he's got that black muzzle and ears? Were you thinking of a name? I hadn't heard you call him anything. But then, I haven't—"

Luke grinned, shaking his head.

"What?" Kristen glanced at Amy, who'd come in to take the tray, and then at Luke again. Amy was chuckling.

"I was going to check your blood pressure and your pupils, but I'm not sure that's relevant anymore."

Her little brows wrinkled, but then her eyes widened. "Oh! Because I'm rattling on and on and no one can get a word in?" She let go of his hand, but he caught it and brought it to his mouth for a soft kiss on the back. He turned it over and kissed her palm, and then her wrist, his gaze never leaving hers. "I think it's adorable."

"You do?" Her voice sounded all breathy, and that did funny things to his pulse. And his cock. If they'd been alone, he would have pulled her into his arms and kissed her until they were both breathless. But he made himself let go of her hand, stand up and step away.

"I can see you showered, I hope you were careful to keep your stitches dry. But there's no bandage to change, so, I guess I better go."

She swallowed, and the desire in her eyes gave his ego another boost. "Yeah. Okay."

He bent to kiss her gently on the temple. "But I'll come by tomorrow." He glanced at Amy, who raised a brow. But he'd be damned before Kekoa or anyone would stop him.

"Okay." She breathed the word more than spoke it.

He made to leave when she called to him. "Luke?"

He spun back, his brows raised.

"Thank you for...today."

"Absolutely."

He was out the door before he noticed the mutt had stayed on the bed with the women. No dummy, that dog.

But Luke's condo felt even emptier than it had before. And the night loomed before him like an endless void.

11

KEKOA SPED DOWN MOKULELE Highway on his Ducati, his mind a confused mess. He loved his boat and being on the water, but that was work. When he needed to get away and think, he hopped on his bike and roared away in whatever direction he found himself going.

Did Amy really believe he'd ever hit her? Had he been so arrogant and controlling with her that she feared him?

He poured over every memory he had of them together. He didn't like what he remembered.

Still, she had to have some reason for fearing violence. And he wanted to know everything about her life before he met her. He knew hardly anything about her. And that was his own fault for never bothering to ask.

He needed to talk with her, but he wouldn't disturb her at Tradewinds again. Somehow he had to get her alone and willing to open up to him.

But how many times would she tell him no before he

gave up? She'd only called him today because Kristen asked her to let him know Kristen wouldn't be diving anytime soon.

He knew what he wanted. But he also knew his duty to his *Ohana*. And yet, if Amy were to give him a chance to get to know her, he'd break it off with Mahina right now.

Kanapapiki! He squeezed the brakes hard, pulled over to the side of the road and put a booted foot down. He was ready to choose Amy over his *Ohana*'s honor!

As if he'd been struck in the head with a surfboard, like Kristen, Kekoa felt the revelation slam into his psyche. His gut had known for a long time what his head refused to acknowledge. He had feelings for Amy. And those feelings were real and powerful. From her brazen style of dress to her vivacious smile and her flippant attitude, he was hooked.

That night in the Tradewinds garden, when she'd refused him so spectacularly, he'd become obsessed with having her. At the time he'd chalked it up to the thrill of the hunt. But he knew now he'd been caught by his prey. She was a loyal friend, with a caring heart and a strength of will he admired.

Damn.

Maybe it was time to let his captor know he'd been tamed.

He checked traffic and then pulled back onto the highway, a plan forming in his mind. Now that he knew what he wanted, he couldn't consent to marrying Mahina no matter what happened with Amy. He gunned the engine and slowed his Ducati only to exit into the town of Puunene, his hometown.

Once a thriving sugar-plantation town, Puunene now consisted mainly of a post office and the Sugar Museum.

Though it was barely over twenty minutes from Kamaole to Puunene, Kekoa didn't visit often—as his parents liked to remind him. He preferred his houseboat on the marina. No commute. And no disapproving parents either. But he was almost thirty years old. It was time to claim his independence.

And then claim his woman.

AMY KICKED HER SHOES off the minute she walked into her house. Her shirt came next, off over the head and tossed wherever it landed on her way to her bedroom. Then her skirt and bra. The trail of dirty clothes was a sarcastic salute to her ex, who'd once broken her jaw for leaving her shoes out.

Now she could clean if she wanted to, or not, if she didn't feel like it right at that moment. And, at this moment, all she wanted was a hot bubble bath and a mug of hot chocolate. With whipped cream. She'd spent the past two days alternating between checking in with Kristen in the afternoon—although that felt unnecessary with Luke there all the time—and then working shorthanded at Tradewinds in the evening.

She started the water running in the tub, added honey-vanilla bath salts and then donned her short silk robe to go make her cocoa. As she put the water on to boil she heard a deep rumbling engine approach until it was in front of her very tiny rented bungalow.

Her heart started pumping faster and her stomach flip-flopped more times than a politician's opinions. Kekoa.

How did he know she was home? She'd spent the last two days and nights at Kristen's when she wasn't waitressing. But Kristen was up and around now, and Luke was there a lot…

The hairs on Amy's neck stood up and she shivered. Had Kekoa been following her? She wasn't frightened or weirded out. Despite Kekoa's imposing manner, she felt instinctively that he lived by a code of honor. And that honor would never allow him to bully someone weaker than himself.

At Kristen's the other night, she'd just been reacting to the stress of the situation. But she really hadn't wanted to reveal that sad story to Kekoa.

He banged on her door and she remembered she wore only her robe and thong. Maybe if she didn't answer he'd think she wasn't home and go away. Oh, her car was out front. He knocked again.

Too bad her new dog was still staying with Kristen.

She padded over to the front door, slipped the safety chain on and opened it just a crack. "Kekoa. It's late and I'm exhausted. Can we please—"

His hand shot up to hold the door open. "Please, listen? Give me three minutes?"

Amy sighed. "Okay."

His stern expression relaxed but he didn't attempt to come inside. He cleared his throat. "One, I broke my engagement to Mahina. Two, I want you more than I've ever wanted anything. And three, I will never hurt you, or try to control you or take away your independence. And to prove it—" he held a large roll of duct tape through the door opening "—you can tape me to a chair while we talk. We don't have to have sex. I just want a chance to get to know you. But if you tell me to leave you alone from now on, I'll respect that." He held his hands out in front of him, wrists together as if he were waiting for a police officer to handcuff him.

Amy blinked a couple of times as his words sunk in. Glancing between the tape and Kekoa with his hands extended… It was ridiculous. She was supposed to bind him up and, what? Have a conversation?

Hell, if she was going to go to all the trouble of duct-taping his hands and feet…

She pictured him naked, lying on her bed, with his hands duct-taped above him. He'd be helpless to her every whim. She could do whatever she wanted to him and he'd have to take it.

Pushing the idea aside, she licked her lips and tried to bring rational thought back to her brain.

Other than experiencing a fantastic night of sex, what would that solve? Wait a minute. What had number one been? He'd broken off his engagement? For her? Amy blinked away water in her eyes. And he wanted to talk. It sounded as though he wanted more than sex.

Actually, if sex with her was all he'd wanted, he'd already had that. That ship had sailed. Been there already. She was getting loopy, maybe high on the endorphins of imagining Kekoa at her mercy sexually....

The piercing whistle of her teakettle made her jump. "Hold on." She ran to the kitchen—which was only about five steps away—lifted the kettle off the burner and turned the stove off.

When she rushed back to her door, Kekoa still stood there, hands extended, wrists together. He could've reached inside the door, slid the chain off the lock and come inside if he'd wanted to. Oh, for heaven's sake. She slid the chain off and opened the door wider. "Come in."

He hesitated, but eventually dropped his hands and stepped forward. Amy glanced out the door before shutting it and leaning against it.

"Do you have water running somewhere?"

"Oh, my gosh! My bath!" She raced back to her bathroom and shut off the water. But already, honey-vanilla water flooded the floor. "Great. Just great."

"Put me to work," Kekoa offered.

By the time they'd soaked up the water with old beach towels and sheets, the bathwater had cooled and so had Amy's mood.

She looked over at Kekoa on his hands and knees. His jeans were soaked from the knees down, and his biceps bunched with every swipe of the towel. A trickle of sweat ran down his temple, but his entire focus was on getting that last bit of water from behind the toilet.

What kind of man did that?

Blake would never have helped her clean up. Just the opposite. He would've slapped her around—at the very least—for making such a mess and wasting water that he paid for with his hard-earned money.

Why was she thinking of Blake?

She leaned against the tub, suddenly aware that her robe didn't cover much of her. And if she were bent over, it probably gaped down the front, too. Yet he hadn't so much as leered. Much less made a move on her. "Thank you."

He sat back on his boot heels, dropped the dripping towel into a laundry basket, and shrugged. "It's my fault this happened."

His humility was almost as powerful an aphrodisiac as the way his gaze smoldered when it traveled down her body. She thought of his wanting to talk. Why not? She had nothing to lose, as far as she could tell. He could talk till the cows came home and she'd never give up her independence again. But that didn't mean they couldn't have a little fun and companionship for as long as it lasted.

"Did you really mean it? You broke off that engagement?"

His back straightened and he lifted his chin. "Yes."

Amy swallowed. Was she really going to do this? "Then let's go to the bedroom." Wow. She was.

His eyes flared. "I didn't come here tonight just for that."

"I know."

"Amy, there's so much I want to learn about you."

"You will. There's time." She got to her feet and held out her hand. His gaze traveled up her legs, lingered on her breasts beneath the silk and finally met her eyes. He took her hand and rose as gracefully as the panther he reminded her of.

As she led him to her bedroom, her breathing quickened. She sat on the edge of the bed and crossed her legs. "Undress for me."

Without hesitation he bent and tugged off one boot, then the other. The thunk of each boot as it hit the hardwood floor matched the pounding of her heart. As if in a trance she watched him peel his T-shirt off over his head and then unzip his jeans and shove them and his underwear down his legs and step out of them.

He was standing naked before her, for her. Her stomach fluttered. His eyes met hers and never looked away while she studied his body.

Oh, my.

They'd made love on his boat. She'd felt the strength of those muscles in his arms when they wrapped around her, lifted her, but the vision before her was breathtaking. The dark, honey-brown skin rippled with defined abs and bulging biceps. His narrow hips emphasized long, thick thighs. And the cock standing at attention between them. She'd felt his hard length inside her. But she'd never actually gotten to see the total package in all its glory.

She slipped the silky robe off her shoulders, and his murmured appreciation sent a jolt of need through her. Then she wiggled out of her thong, lay down and gestured for him to join her, patting the bed.

Though she could tell he wanted to pounce, he crawled up slowly and lay beside her.

She climbed on top of him, straddling his hips, with his thick, standing cock primed for her. But she didn't touch it yet. Instead, she pushed his arms above his head. Mmm, that position stretched his torso and lifted his rib cage. It rose and fell as he took a deep breath. He licked his lips and she wanted to lick them, too. Lick everywhere. She leaned forward and kissed him, licking and nipping at his lips at first before taking his mouth in hers and plunging her tongue deep.

He moaned and moved beneath her, but she was careful to keep her stomach from rubbing his cock. So many places to kiss, so little time. Her lips traveled down his jaw to his collarbone and lower until she reached a flat brown nipple. Taking it between her teeth, she teased it and licked it, and enjoyed the sounds coming from deep in his throat.

Her hands had been busy caressing his muscular shoulders and biceps, and now she ran her palms down his chest, relishing the firmness, the hills and valleys of every muscle down his abdomen, and finally coming to his dark, hard cock.

She swiped the bead of moisture at the tip with a finger and trailed it down his length. He inhaled and twitched. She lifted her gaze to Kekoa's eyes. He stared at her with a mixture of awe and pleading.

"Amy, *E Ku'u Aloha.*" The pitch of his voice had deepened and he sounded a bit strangled.

"You said that the other day. What does it mean?"

His expression softened and he gave her a small smile. "My love."

Her throat tightened, but she shoved the emotion down. It was just a saying. "Say something else in Hawaiian. It's a beautiful language."

He full-out grinned. *"Honi ko'u ule."*

She raised a brow. "I know *honi* means kiss."

"Kiss my cock."

She crossed her arms. "That sounds very controlling."

He lost his grin and growled. "Please?"

"Well, since you asked nicely." She lowered her head and took him into her mouth slowly, enjoying how he groaned and writhed his hips. When she looked up at him he was gritting his teeth. "I'm just getting started, Kekoa." She smirked.

His expression became impassive and his gaze went to the ceiling. She couldn't have that, so she sucked him deep and fast, pumping him with her lips.

He grunted and groaned and, finally, he shifted his

hips away from her. "Please. I don't want to come that way."

"Lucky for you, I don't want you to either." She brought his arms down to his sides.

"Yes, thank the gods." He sounded truly tortured. His hands clenched and unclenched. "I want to touch you."

With a secret smile, she leaned over to the bedside-table drawer, opened it and grabbed a handful of condoms. Her breasts brushed his chest and he arched his back to push up against them.

While she was leaning down anyway, she kissed him, lips moving over his, deeper this time, telling him she was done teasing. She curled her arms around his head and moaned, herself, as he took control of the kiss, raising his head and exploring her tongue with his. This is what she wanted. This is what turned her on.

She didn't need complete control to feel safe with Kekoa. She needed the respect and the freedom to choose. And if she had her choice, what really turned her on was Kekoa's inner strength, his moral code.

"Amy?"

Her thoughts returned to the moment. She'd stopped kissing him as she acknowledged the truth. "I do trust you, Kekoa. I think I've known since we met that you were...an honorable man."

Emotion seized his expression. "Amy." He reached up to stroke a long strand of her hair, and then lifted his head to gently kiss her lips, her cheek, just below her ear.

Sighing, she shifted onto her back, her arms circling her head. "Make love to me, Kekoa."

With a strangled groan, he rolled to his side and trailed a hand down her throat to her collarbone, between her breasts to her stomach, then returned by the same path with the back of his fingers. His palm found one breast and cupped her tenderly, lifting the nipple to his mouth. His tongue teased, his lips suckled, and when he had her writhing and whimpering, he moved to the next one, leaving a trail of kisses in his wake.

His hand drifted lazily down to find her sensitive clit and worked in tandem with his mouth to bring her to the brink.

So lost in sensation was she that she barely registered a tearing noise and looked up to see he'd opened one of the condom wrappers. Kekoa slipped between her thighs. Then he stilled.

"What?" She cradled his cheek in her palm.

"You're still in control. Tell me you want this as much as I do." His jaw tightened as he stared hard into her eyes.

Feeling so gloriously happy made her mischievous. "Hmm. Maybe."

"Amy! Don't torment me anymore." His features softened. "Please."

Smiling, she wrapped her legs around his waist,

hooked her ankles and pushed her hips up to rub against him. "Yes. I want you. Now."

Before she'd finished speaking he reared back and pushed inside her to the hilt. She gasped and moaned and he brought his mouth to hers and kissed her passionately, possessively. His mouth, his hands, his cock all built an exquisite pressure until she cried out and they climaxed together. She'd never felt so sated, so at peace.

Powerful emotions overcame her and she squeezed her eyes to stop the tears. She'd never been able to tease, to play, to be herself during lovemaking. Peace and acceptance filled her and she tightened her arms around Kekoa. She'd never felt this kind of intimacy with a man.

"Amy," Kekoa murmured into her neck as he tried to catch his breath. He lifted his head to look into her eyes. "I'm not expecting anything. But I want us to see where this might go."

Fear and joy battled for supremacy inside her. She wasn't ready for a commitment. But she wanted to be with Kekoa. "As long as we can take it slow."

His arms tightened around her and he kissed her, fiercely, as if he had to pour everything he felt into the kiss before she changed her mind. But she wouldn't.

Afterward, they refilled the bathtub and climbed in together, soaping and pleasuring each other's bodies. She lay back against his chest and he had to raise his knees to fit.

"Amy?" He paused, a hand resting on her stomach. "Your ex. He hit you?"

Amy stilled, her fingers frozen where she'd been stroking Kekoa's thigh. "Yes."

His hand curled into a fist. "More than once?"

She swallowed. "Yes."

"How long were you with him?"

"Kekoa. It's over now. I'm free."

"How long?"

"Six years. But—"

"*Kanapapiki!* I'd like to kill that son of a bitch!" He wrapped his arms around her and buried his nose in her neck. "I wish I'd been there to protect you."

"It's okay that you weren't. I'm not helpless. I don't need a big he-man to come in and save me. I got myself in it, and I got myself out of it."

"Is he in jail?"

"Are you kidding? He got worse than jail. Before I left Mississippi, I made sure his mamma, his daddy, his grandmamma, his boss and his new girlfriend all received photos of me the last time he laid into me."

"You recorded something like that?"

"I had to. It would've just been my word against his in court. And even after I moved out, he stalked me, so I knew he wasn't going to go peacefully."

She felt him shake his head behind her. "*You're* amazing." He kissed her from her neck to her shoulder.

"Speaking of mammas. Did you tell your parents about breaking off your engagement?"

He grunted into her shoulder. "I couldn't believe it. I sat them down and made my announcement...and they just looked at each other and shrugged. They told me Mahina had told her parents she refused to marry me and had left for the mainland back in September to go to Harvard."

Amy laughed. "Go, Mahina."

"Yes, but could it have killed someone to inform me?"

Amy giggled at his disgruntled tone but he caught her mouth in his. Kissing turned into caressing and soon Kekoa lifted her into his strong arms and carried her back to bed.

A long while later, they lay in each other's arms. Amy was almost asleep when she thought about Kristen. She was worried about her friend. Visiting her the last couple of days, Amy had noticed Kristen becoming more and more withdrawn. The quiet sadness was so unlike her outgoing, optimistic friend. But when Amy asked her about it, Kristen only mumbled something about the contest being over for her.

Amy mentioned it to Kekoa. He confirmed that she'd canceled her rental of his boat and his services. But he didn't know how to help Kristen any more than she did.

12

"GET UP, LAZY HEAD." Luke yanked open the blinds in her bedroom.

Kristen groaned and pulled the pillow over her face. "Go away."

"Come on, Kristen, You've spent three days in this bed. You're supposed to rest, but this is extreme. And it's not like you."

Irritation bubbled into anger. She sat up and slammed the pillow on the mattress. "How do you know what I'm like?"

The dog whined.

"God, you're beautiful when you're mad." He stood in front of the window, even in silhouette, as handsome as ever, holding a large store-bought coffee cup.

She brought the pillow back up to cover her face. "I'm disgusting." She had bed hair and morning breath, hairy legs and a small, shaved bump on her head. But even on a good day she wouldn't call herself beautiful.

He came around and sat on the bed beside her, offering the coffee. The rich aroma tantalized her senses as she took the cup. "You couldn't be if you tried."

She scowled, and set the coffee on the table. "Don't be nice. Then I'll have to be nice and I don't want to."

"You don't have to be nice." He reached up and softly brushed away a tangle of hair.

"Oh, Luke."

He got to his feet, wrenched the covers off her and grabbed her around the waist. "But you do have to get out of bed." He hauled her up and carried her—as she screamed and fought him—to the bathroom. Ooh! He would not get away with this!

"Now." He set her down in front of the vanity. "You can either shower on your own or—" he reached around her and swiped back the shower curtain "—I can assist you."

She folded her arms and glared at him. "Fine. May I have some privacy, please?" she ground out between gritted teeth.

"Promise you'll shower?"

"What do you care, anyway?"

"We have someplace to be by noon." He glanced at the watch on his wrist. "So, get a move on."

"Someplace to be? Where—"

He reached for her again.

"Okay, okay. Geez."

He grinned, turned and left her to her privacy.

After showering and shaving and brushing her teeth,

she felt more like a human again and padded out to the living room. The empty living room. Wow, the depression she thought she'd left in the shower came back full force as she realized Luke was gone.

The lock rattled, the door opened and Luke strolled in with Blackbeard on a leash. The dog bounced until Luke removed his leash, and then trotted into the kitchen for water.

Kristen's mood improved. She smiled. "I thought you'd left."

"I did leave." He hung the leash on the doorknob. "But I came back." He smiled.

He had the best smile. All the more beautiful because it was so rare. "So, where are we going?"

"It's a surprise. First, tell me what's wrong."

The depression, never really gone, popped back up to the surface. "I can't dive for two weeks. At least, not deep diving. And the contest deadline is a week from today and I've got nothing."

It was silly to cry over something like this after what she'd been through. But she'd put a lot of things on the line for this chance to make her dream come true. And the worst of it was she'd brought it on herself all because of some deep need to prove the threat of dying—of her cancer recurring—wouldn't stop her from living her life. But prove it to whom? Seems she hadn't made peace with her brush with death like she thought she had.

"Maybe you have it and don't know it. Can I see your photos again?"

She blinked, unaccustomed to this optimistic Luke. Was he just feeling guilty? He'd been wonderful ever since her accident. Which made it even harder to keep her guard up around him. Who was she kidding? She'd never been good at separating herself and her emotions.

Rubbing her wet eyes, she sniffed. "Okay." She headed for the kitchen table and he followed, sitting beside her while she opened her laptop. Just like last time, she brought up her contest photos and passed the laptop to him. "There you go."

Several minutes of silence went by while Luke scrolled through her photos. She took the occasion to study him, as fascinated by him as the night they'd met.

He'd shaved, and he smelled divine. That fresh masculine scent she'd always associate with him. His cargo shorts and T-shirt were neat and clean. Today he wore a gray U.S. Army Medical Corps T-shirt that clung to the slopes and planes of his hard chest. While he studied the photos, he rubbed his jaw, or raised his brows quickly, but mostly he was silent.

He was a quiet man. A man who took action when it was needed, like saving that tourist in Tradewinds, or getting her discharged when she wanted to leave the hospital. But he also had an inherent stillness in him, maybe *calmness* was a good word. A quality that would come in handy in a frantic setting like an E.R., or a military hospital during a bombing.

He sat back in the chair. "I pulled out a few I thought were contenders. You've got some amazing shots, Kristen." His gaze landed on her and though his normal expression rarely changed, she sensed he wanted to ask her something.

"What?"

"Can I see them now? The ones you didn't want me to see before?"

She rolled her bottom lip in and bit it. They'd made love. And yet, letting him see her personal pictures seemed an extreme act of intimacy. If they upset him, he might reject her again. Which sounded ridiculous with the carnage he had to have witnessed in Afghanistan. And what did she have to lose? In a week's time, they'd both go their separate ways and never see each other again.

With a deep breath, she leaned over to open her personal photos folder and then sat back, arms folded.

He didn't move for a second, and then he ran the back of his hand down her cheek. "Thank you."

At her quick nod he turned his attention to the laptop and the photos no one else had seen except her mom.

The collection was a photographic diary of her life during her fight with cancer. From the day of the biopsy, to the disturbingly graphic post-op photos of her mastectomy, all were incredibly personal. She looked over at Luke, wincing ahead of time at his reaction.

His eyes were filled with tears, but every once in a while his mouth would curve in a tiny smile. She glanced over. Ah, the day she'd shaved her head and went to try on wigs—from long dreadlocks to a flaming-red afro, she'd had fun being silly with her mom that day.

Kristen noticed he hadn't moved his fingers over the touchpad, or clicked to the next picture in a while. She leaned in to see what he was staring at. Oh, God. One of the worst. Not because it was graphic, it wasn't. But it represented probably her worst day, emotionally. The only time suicide had ever been a viable option, even if only for a few minutes.

It was, like a lot of them, a self-portrait. But it was a close-up of mostly her face looking directly into the mirror. Her hair was long gone in that photo, and she'd been puking for days. Reconstruction seemed a lifetime away and in the meantime she'd felt like a lopsided freak.

And tired. So tired. Of fighting. Of feeling like a burden to her family. Her eyes were sunken, and bloodshot, and her lips were cracked and bleeding, and she'd been so weak she could barely hold the camera up. But she'd wanted to remember the day, so she could look back for the rest of her life and be reminded not to sweat the small stuff.

Luke raised an arm and wiped his eyes on his sleeve. He cleared his throat. "The contest has different categories, right?"

"Yes, three. People, places and nature."

He looked over at her.

"No. I didn't even want *you* to see that."

"It's the one, Kristen. You said it yourself, the winner has to be unique. There's no other photo like that on earth."

Maybe so, but there was no way. She shook her head, feeling panicky all of a sudden. "Luke. I can't. I appreciate your input, but…" She gulped in air.

Luke gently shut the laptop, took her shoulders and turned her toward him. "It's okay. You don't have to." He scooped her up and set her on his lap, holding her against him. "You don't have to do anything you don't want to do, okay?"

She let out a deep breath and nodded, and he cupped the back of her head while he pressed a soft kiss to her temple.

With a whimper, Kristen wrapped her arms around his neck, turned and straddled his legs and kissed him on the mouth, hungry, starving for that indefinable thing human contact provides. That feeling of being alive, and in the moment, and being a part of something bigger than oneself.

His arms tightened around her and he returned her kiss, just as deep, just as desperate. "Kristen." He angled his head, took control of the kiss, long and lingering. His hands ran over her body, squeezing her bottom, cupping her breast, cradling her face as he pulled away, breathing hard. "Let's continue this once we get there." He grasped her waist, lifted her and set her on her feet, and then stood.

Still dazed by passion, she clung to his shoulders. "Are you sure you don't want to just stay here?"

"Trust me. You'll be glad you went. Now—" he grinned, took her shoulders and steered her toward her bedroom "—put a swimsuit on under your clothes, and wear a good pair of hiking shoes." He held up a backpack. "Put whatever else you want to bring in here."

Kristen grumbled all the way back to her bedroom. All she wanted to do was crawl back in bed and make love with Luke until it was time to leave for home. It was kind of fun getting to be the grouchy one.

TURNED OUT THERE WAS no easy way to get from where they were on the island to the Haleakala National Park. At least that was what the kind lady at the visitor's information center had told Luke. She'd provided a map and a few landmarks, but that was it.

What might have taken thirty minutes as the crow flies took almost two hours of backtracking north and then traveling all the way around to the south coast, driving down winding roads that twisted this way and that. Luke would've enjoyed the astoundingly gorgeous scenery more if he'd been sure of finding his destination.

Misty volcanic mountains covered in lush greenery fenced them in on the north side and a coastline of sparkling Pacific Ocean to the south. When there was no one else on the road, which there frequently wasn't, one could feel a sense of timelessness about the place. And Kristen at least seemed to be enjoying the drive.

But at last Luke pulled the Jeep into the general-store parking lot the visitor's guide had mentioned.

Kristen jumped out of the Jeep and stretched, then met him at the store's door and threw her arms around his waist. She looked up at him with her beautiful smile and a light in her blue eyes that made everything worth it. "I'm going to the ladies' room. I'll meet you at the counter." She swished off. He loved that view. The cute little butt in the shorts.

Luke made himself look away and went to check his directions with the store attendant. After he hit the latrine, he met Kristen at the counter. She had a few energy bars and an ice cream bar. He pulled out his wallet, but she covered it with her hand. "I got this. You want anything?"

"Besides you?"

She blinked up at him, eyes wide. "Why, Captain Andrews, aren't you the brazen one." The teasing smile faded and her face softened to a sensual yearning so potent he almost carried her off right then.

But what else he had in mind would be so much better.

Within a couple of minutes they were back in the Jeep, making their way up Piilani Highway to the Kipahulu area. From there they parked and the hike was supposed to be less than a mile. When they crossed a bridge and Luke saw the sign for the Alelele stream, he knew he was on track.

Ten minutes later, the narrow path, closed in by thick

forest, opened up, and he could hear the roar of the falls. When he pushed a large palm frond out of the way, the most gloriously beautiful sight appeared before him. White water cascaded about a hundred feet down a narrow black-rock formation into a clear, secluded pond.

"Oh, Luke." Kristen's voice held a reverence as she stood beside him, taking in the scene. She spun to face him. "Thank you." She reached up, cradled his face in her hands and kissed him briefly on the lips. Then she shoved him in the chest. "You snooze, you lose." With a mischievous wrinkle of her nose, she climbed down the embankment, sometimes stumbling, using her hands until she'd reached the edge of the water.

He scrambled down after her, catching up just as she pulled her second shoe and sock off and tossed them onto the grassy slope. She shimmied out of her shorts to reveal a tiny pink bikini bottom.

His libido went on high alert. Kristen in a bikini. His heart racing, he yanked his T-shirt off and tossed it behind him, and then toed out of his running shoes. But he stopped when Kristen waded into the pool with her T-shirt still on.

What the…?

"Ooh, Luke, it's fantastic." The roar of the falls was so loud she had to raise her voice for him to hear her. She twisted at the waist and gestured for him to join her. "Come on."

Still in his shorts, he stared at her. This was unacceptable. He shucked off his shorts and then, on impulse, slid his briefs off, too.

"Luke! What if someone else shows up?" She backed away as he waded in and got close—smart girl. Maybe she could read the determination in his face.

"There's no one else around. Take off your T-shirt, Kristen."

"I'm fine the way I am, thank you."

He kept approaching and she kept backing up until she was treading water to stay afloat, while he still had traction in the sandy bottom. "I want to see you. All of you." He lunged for her, but she squealed and splashed away.

Arms stroking through the water, she swam to the other side of the pond and turned around to face him. "You have already."

Chasing her in the water was fun, but he'd hoped to share this day differently. "Kristen. Come here."

Uncertainty crossed her features. She looked so vulnerable. He held his arms out. "Just let me hold you."

She gave him a tremulous smile and swam toward him. He swam toward her and once the distance closed between them he gathered her into his arms and twirled with her in the water.

With a groan, he covered her mouth with his as he'd been wanting to ever since they'd left the condo. Her arms were around his neck and her legs wrapped around his waist. No way she could miss his erection. He loved the way her fingers curled into his hair as he moved his mouth over hers, deeper and deeper still, their bodies touching. But he wanted her skin touching his.

He'd take the next best thing. He slid his hands under her shirt, caressing the soft skin of her back and cupping her cute bikini-clad bottom. His lips found their way down her throat, but the damn T-shirt was in the way. He lifted his head, frustrated.

She pushed out of his arms and swam for shore.

Damn, now he'd ruined it. "Kristen, wait."

But she didn't get out, just grabbed the hem of her T-shirt and pulled it up and over her head and tossed it onto the rocks surrounding the pond. As she faced him, her chin raised, and even if the uncertainty had returned, she deliberately reached behind her and unhooked her bikini top. She pulled it off and tossed it behind her.

As she stood so brave, yet so vulnerable, her arms held to her sides, Luke raced to shore to hold her. Her body wasn't all curves and fullness, but petite and toned. Her breasts were small, the nipples tiny little buds, and the reconstructed breast would never quite match the one nature made. But that just made her beauty all the more unique and captivating.

The reddened, raised scars were much more visible in the bright sunlight, even from this distance, but she was so strong, so courageous, he wanted to make her his forever.

He'd never met a woman like her, and he knew he

never would again. She was everything he loved and everything he wanted. Everything he needed.

Reaching her, he took her into his arms and pulled her tight against him. He slipped his hand beneath her bikini bottom and tugged it down her legs and off, leaving it on the rocky shore. Then he carried her back out to the middle of the pool and beneath the spray of the waterfall itself.

All the while he kissed her everywhere. Her ear, her neck, her shoulder. He lifted her arm and reverently kissed along each scar, under her breast, finally taking the nipple between his lips. She didn't react and he realized she hadn't last time, and moved his lips to the other nipple.

Kristen gasped, dropped her head back and clutched his head as he licked and teased the nipple with his tongue. Her reaction drove him wild. Her stomach rubbed against his cock, and her hands were all over him, kneading, caressing.

It'd been a week since he'd made love to her, been inside her, and he needed to be again. Now. Lifting her leg to his hip, he slid his fingers between her thighs and through the small folds, testing her readiness.

She moaned and moved her hips, pressing into his fingers.

"Protection?" he rasped.

"I'm all right. You?"

"I am, too. We're okay, then?"

"Mmm." She nodded. "Now." She wiggled her hips.

He cupped her butt and lifted her over his straining cock. She hooked her legs around his waist and sank onto him, her eyes locked with his.

He had to grit his teeth and hold her still a moment or else embarrass himself. She was so hot and tight around him. He closed his eyes until the need to move overwhelmed him.

Groaning, he lost all control. Caught up in the exquisite sensation, he thrust into her over and over. She moved her hips against him, making unintelligible noises.

As he neared climax he sought her gaze again, trying to hold on until she was ready. She met his look and nodded. He let go and shuddered, so in awe of Kristen. Lost in a profound connection with her.

When he could breathe again, he opened his eyes and realized he was leaning against a rock beside the cascade of falls. Kristen was still clinging to his neck and waist, her head tucked beneath his chin. "You okay?"

"Mmm, perfect. Let's stay here forever."

And that was the subject neither one of them had brought up. "Kristen, do you..." He wanted to ask her if she ever saw herself living the life of an army wife. Although the medical corps tended to get stationed stateside in one place and stay there, there would always be a war somewhere.

But wasn't it too soon? They'd only known each other a few weeks. He thought what he felt was real, but he might as well be on Fantasy Island right now, given how close this place was to real life. She'd think he was crazy.

"Do I what?" She lifted her head and gazed at him.

"Do you want something to eat?"

She blinked and something flickered in her eyes. Disappointment? Sadness?

Whatever it was, he felt a sense of missed opportunity.

She disentangled herself from him and the cool water hit what had been surrounded by warmth. He hissed and watched her swim for shore. Worried, he followed.

Once she reached the backpack, she pulled a beach towel from it, dried off and then slipped on her bikini bottoms and her T-shirt. He wanted to tell her, *No. Wrap only in the towel and let me hold you skin to skin,* but he stayed silent and wrapped a towel around his waist.

She pulled out her camera and started snapping pictures. The falls, the pond, their surroundings. And finally him.

"Oh, no." He shook his head, hating to have his picture taken. "Kristen."

"These will stay private, Luke. I promise. These are just for me."

"Will you let me take a few of you and will you send them to me?"

Her smile was warm with a hint of melancholy to it. "I'd like that."

"All right." He propped his forearms on his knees and looked into the camera as she clicked the button over and over, circling him and getting different angles. "Okay, that's plenty." He held up a hand. "My turn."

Pouting, she handed it over. He stood and had her sit on a rock with the falls behind her. He checked the viewfinder screen and then looked back at her. "I don't suppose I could get you to take off your—"

"Luke! No." But she was smiling.

"No, I only meant you could hold it up in front of you."

"Oh." He could see her internal debate. Her face was so expressive. And he saw the moment she decided to do it. Once she had the shirt safely covering her, he started snapping photos. And once he was taking pictures she slowly blossomed into a seductive siren, posing more and more provocatively until finally she looked directly into the camera and he could swear she was telling him she loved him with her eyes.

He clicked the picture and then looked over the camera directly at her, but her gaze darted away and the moment was gone.

She retrieved her camera from him and returned it to the backpack, then pulled out a couple of energy bars, but she didn't even open the packages. She lay back with her hands behind her head and closed her eyes. After several seconds of silence, she said, "Would you tell me more about yourself, Luke? Where'd you grow up? What's your family like? What do you do when you're not doctoring or staying on Maui?"

He moved to lie beside her. As opposed to the last time she asked about him, he didn't feel in the spotlight. He felt grateful she wanted to know. "I'm from a small town in West Texas. You've never heard of it."

"Tell me anyway?"

"Rankin. Population about eight hundred. Closest big city is Odessa."

"And your dad drove a truck. What did your mom do?"

"She stayed home until dad died. Then she went back to teaching. I think that was hardest on my baby brother. He was only three and suddenly he was going to a daycare all day."

"How many brothers and sisters?"

"Two of each. I'm the oldest. Then my brother James. Then the girls and my baby brother."

"Wow. Five kids."

She said the word *five* as though it was dreadful. "You don't want kids?"

"Sure, but probably not five."

Crazy relief hit his gut. As if she'd ever want a life with a guy who couldn't even sleep through the night without waking up, screaming, in a cold sweat.

"Do you? Want kids?"

More than anything he wanted a wife, kids, a home.

Happy. Normal. "Yes." Could she hear the desperate longing in that word like he could?

He caught her nodding from the corner of his eye. "What about your brothers and sisters? Where are they now?"

"Both my sisters married and teach in Rankin. My mom loves having her grandkids close by. My baby brother is still in college. And James is in the Army, too. He flies a helicopter and is serving in Afghanistan." It was the one thing he dreaded most. He wasn't sure he could remain sane if he saw his brother come into his hospital in Kabul. An image from his most recent nightmare flashed through his psyche, bloody and chaotic. The mangled soldier in his nightmare was his brother.

He must've flinched or made some noise, because when he blinked Kristen had rolled to lie half over him, stroking his face. "Luke? It's okay."

He wrenched her into his arms and held her tight, hiding his face in her shoulder. She held him until he got his trembling under control, then he rolled her beneath him and kissed her, so desperately, longing for what couldn't be.

They kissed and snuggled on the grassy embankment, taking all time they wanted to explore each other's body and touch and caress. They swam and made love in the water again until there was more shade than sun.

When they got out to dry off, Luke dug the earrings

out of the backpack, knelt beside her and gave them to her.

"Oh, Luke."

He took the earrings out and gently put them on her. Before he'd finished, she started crying and he held her, his throat tight. But twilight was fast approaching. He hadn't packed flashlights, so they loaded up and, holding hands, made their way back to the Jeep. As if it might break the spell, neither one of them spoke.

Just as it got full dark, he started the engine, turned on his headlights and backed out onto the highway. They had a long drive home.

Somewhere along the coastline on Piilani Highway they pulled up behind a slow-moving tour bus. Luke backed off, not in a hurry to get back anyway. He was hungry. Maybe they'd stop and have some dinner somewhere along the way. The more he thought about it, the hungrier he got. He turned to look at Kristen, opened his mouth to suggest the idea to her.

"Luke!" Horror filled Kristen's face and she pointed ahead of them.

The tour bus swerved off the road and Luke had to stomp on his brakes to avoid a cyclist lying in the road. He stopped in time, but the bus wasn't able to. With a devastating crunch of metal and human screams, it went down the steep cliff, tipped over and rolled down to the rocky shore.

13

KRISTEN UNCLICKED HER seat belt and jumped from the Jeep. Her stomach was knotted in horror. She'd never witnessed anything like this.

Luke put the Jeep in Park, punched the hazard lights button and followed her.

The guy on the bicycle was already getting to his feet, brushing himself off. He wore a helmet and his bike had a headlight, but it was a winding road. He must have rounded the curve and the bus driver didn't see him in time. Luke examined the cyclist, but he'd lucked out. Only a sprained wrist and some bad scrapes on the guy's legs.

While Luke helped the bicyclist move out of the road, she steeled herself to look over the edge of the cliff and down. *Oh, my God.* The bus was on its side, crushed in on all sides. People were screaming, some trying to get out. Others had been thrown from the bus and lay scattered like rag dolls across the shore. A few moving, most not.

They had to help those people. But it wouldn't do anyone any good to panic. Kristen ran back to the Jeep, dug her cell out of the backpack and punched in 9-1-1. She was shaking so hard it was difficult to talk. And trying to describe where they were… Thank goodness her phone had a GPS.

Luke was rummaging in the back of the Jeep and came around to the front carrying a small first-aid kit. He pulled out everything from the backpack except the beach towels and the bottled water and stuck the first-aid kit in, then pulled the backpack on and headed for the cliff's edge.

"Luke! Wait!"

He spun to face her.

Just climbing down that cliff was going to be dangerous. Especially in the dark. "We need light."

He gave a quick nod.

The only source of light was the battery-powered headlight from the bike. Luke disconnected it and stuck it in his backpack, also. Kristen moved the Jeep to face the ocean and left the headlights on.

As she approached, Luke took her shoulders. "Wait here for the ambulance."

"No! I'm coming with you. He can wait here." She pointed at the bicyclist. "He can't manage the climb with his wrist anyway."

"Kristen, you don't want to go down there." Luke's

face was grim, hardened. "Please. Stay here." Before she could say anymore, he'd scrambled over the edge and was climbing down the cliff's side.

"Luke!" She wanted to scream her frustration. No way was she waiting here. She might not be a doctor, but she could tie a tourniquet and knew the basics of CPR. Gathering her courage, she started down.

As she hit the bottom and turned to make her way to the bus, the people's screams grew louder. Luke stood a couple of feet away. But he wasn't moving. She reached his side and touched his shoulder. He didn't acknowledge her and his posture was stiff. She moved in front of him. His eyes were squeezed closed.

She knew what was happening. He was having another flashback. "Luke." She shook his shoulder. "Luke, help me. These people need you."

His eyes opened and he focused on her. "I can't save them all, Kristen."

"No. But we have to do what we can. That's all we can do."

He blinked. But he didn't move into action.

"Come on." She dug the headlight out of the backpack, turned it on and shone it on the bus. "Let's get them out." She headed for the bus, stepping carefully over jagged rocks.

Without checking to see if Luke followed, she climbed up onto the bus's side, which was now the top, and started helping people out the windows. She could help leverage some, but she wasn't strong enough to lift the more frail passengers. From behind her, a pair of strong arms reached in a window and lifted an older woman out and lowered her to the ground below.

Luke.

Between the two of them they pulled everyone who was mobile out within a few minutes. While he worked, Luke called orders to those he pulled out. "Tear a long strip off your shirt and use the rest as padding, then use the strip to tie around it and stop that bleeding," he told one man. And to a young woman he ordered, "Lie down and keep your leg elevated."

There were a few still in the bus who were trapped by seats, and a couple who were either unconscious or…dead.

While Kristen held the light, Luke lowered himself in through a window and checked all those not moving. He couldn't lift them out, so he saw to everyone still alive, lifting a seat off one, disentangling limbs. At his request, Kristen lowered down a beach towel, which he made into a neck brace, and he pulled off his own shirt to use as a tourniquet for another.

Assuring them that more help was on the way, Luke climbed back out of the bus and down to the ground. He caught Kristen as she slid down the side. With her holding the light, they made their way from one body to the next, helping those still alive. The bus driver had been thrown the farthest and was beyond help.

Luke remained stoic, almost as if he were on auto-pilot. His expression was unreadable even with the

sound of human suffering all around, whereas Kristen
was crying even as she followed Luke's instructions,
bandaging wounds where she could.

Finally they heard sirens and saw the flashing lights
of several emergency vehicles. Even a medevac helicopter arrived. But Luke continued to help, offering
reports on the ones he'd had to leave in the bus and
staying until everyone was up the cliff and in the hands
of another emergency medical professional.

Exhausted and filthy, Kristen sat in the back of a
police car. She looked around and realized she and
Luke were the only ones left. The police officer was
talking to Luke and writing on a notepad. She didn't
know how Luke was still standing, or even speaking
coherently. All she wanted was a hot shower and to
crawl into bed and never get out. At some point she'd
stopped crying and gone numb.

She must've dozed off because she jerked awake
when the car door opened and Luke slid in next to
her and pulled her into his arms. She thought she was
numb, but she started crying again, and Luke held her
and comforted her until she'd cried it all out. Then they
wearily told the officers goodbye and returned to the
Jeep.

It seemed forever to get home, but she must've fallen
asleep again, because when Luke gently shook her
awake, they were back at the condo. He walked her to
her place, made sure she got inside and then kissed her
on the forehead and headed for the door.

"You're leaving?" She clung to his hand.

"I'm done in."

"Come get in the shower with me."

He hesitated and she used his exhaustion to pull him into the bathroom, undress him and urge him into the shower. Caring for him seemed to give her a burst of energy and she massaged his shoulders and back while she soaped him up.

His moans made it all worth it.

She dropped into the bed beside him, her hair still wrapped in a towel, and fell immediately asleep.

When she woke up, it was daylight, the dog was whining and Luke was gone.

KRISTEN TEXTED AMY, asked her to come over. She needed to talk. Then she texted Luke.

R U OK? Come over?

Amy answered.

Luke didn't.

By the time Kristen was dressed, had walked the dog and made coffee, Amy was there.

And Luke still hadn't answered.

"But he could still be sleeping." She spilled the whole story of the bus crash—and everything that happened before it—to Amy the minute her friend stepped through the door. "I'm exhausted and keyed up at the same time and I didn't deal with half of what he dealt with." She sipped her coffee and grabbed a blueberry muffin from the basket Amy had brought.

"Geez, Kris. I can't even imagine." Amy shuddered. "But still. It's almost two in the afternoon."

Kristen bit her lip. "True. You think I should call him again?"

"No. He'll come to you when he's ready. At least, that's how it worked for me." Amy got a glint in her eye and a secretive smile slowly curved her lips.

"What?"

Her friend's face glowed with happiness. "I don't know if this is the right time to be telling you this, but we've told each other everything these past few months…"

"Tell, tell!" Kristen could use some good news right now. She listened as Amy told her about Kekoa coming over and helping her clean up the mess when the tub overflowed, and how that led to wet clothes and getting out of them… And how Kekoa wanted a relationship with her.

"Oh, Amy, I'm so happy for you." She hugged her friend, meaning every word with all her heart, even if there was a teeny-tiny particle of envy lodged there.

By the time Amy left, taking her new dog with her, Luke still hadn't responded. And Kristen was really worried. Maybe she should wait until he was ready. But patience had never been her strong suit. To hell with waiting for him to come to her. He was two floors up.

With a sense of déjà vu, she knocked on his door.

This time he answered right away. And he looked military sharp. Except for the sunken eyes and the haunted look in their depths. That looked familiar.

And he stood at the door, holding the knob, blocking her entry. "Hey, I'm sorry I haven't called you back." He glanced behind him, then back to her. "I've been really busy."

"Busy? Doing what?" She peered behind him at the large duffel bag sitting by the sofa, and a smaller one beside it.

He drew in a deep breath. "Packing. Look—" he interrupted what she would've said "—I was going to call you later."

"Later?" There was a huge lump in her throat. "Like, from-the-plane later? Or from Texas?"

"No." He shook his head.

"Can I at least come in?"

He hesitated—hesitated!—and then stepped back and opened the door wider.

"We need to talk about last night."

"No, we don't." He did an about-face and headed for the living room.

"Luke, I'm alive right now because the minute I felt that lump in my breast, I made an appointment with a doctor. What if I'd denied its existence? There's nothing wrong with needing a little help to get beyond what you've been through. Anyone who does what you do, and did last night, my God, anyone would need help processing that kind of trauma."

"I'll handle it. Don't worry about me."

"Really? Did you sleep last night?"

His lips tightened. "I've got a plane to catch in Lahaina." He glanced at his watch.

What could she say to that? He'd thrown up a wall of indifference. Switched off his emotions. It was as if the man from yesterday never existed. But she had to try one last time to tell him how she felt. Otherwise, she'd regret it the rest of her life. "Luke. Over the past few weeks, I've—"

"Don't."

"Don't?"

"Kristen. I've had fun the past couple of weeks with you, but we knew going in, it was a vacation thing. You have your life to go back to. I have mine."

If only that were true. Then her heart wouldn't be hurting right now. But she'd done something incredibly stupid. She'd fallen in love. If she hadn't known it before yesterday, she knew it for sure last night as she watched him pull himself from the brink and do what had to be done. "Luke, I'm trying to tell you I lo—"

"Kristen, you're making this a lot harder on both of us than it has to be." He strode to the door and held it open for her. "I wish you all the best."

She stood there, blinking back tears. But she wasn't going to throw herself at his feet. She had some pride. Chin up, she met him at the door and looked into his eyes one last time. "Goodbye, Luke."

Her vision blurred, she stumbled a little down the

hallway to the elevator. She'd take what was left of her shredded heart and go home. She couldn't dive until after the contest deadline. That was why she'd moved to Maui in the first place. And right now, she wanted her mom and dad. She wanted to curl up in her bedroom at home and be a little girl again with all her life ahead of her just waiting to happen exactly like she wanted it to.

But she'd survived worse than the crushing pain she felt right now. And she'd survive again. During the flight back to San Diego, she studied her photos on her laptop and set aside the best ones she thought might have even the slightest chance of winning the Nature category. Then she found herself opening the personal photos folder and committing masochism by looking at the pictures from Alelele Falls.

How could a man she'd known only a few weeks come to mean so much to her? She wanted to throttle him with her bare hands. And she wanted to kiss him until he knew how much she loved him. She wanted to tell him he was a hero for what he did for the bus crash victims. And she wanted to tell him heroes had limitations just like lesser mortals.

When the older gentleman beside her handed her his handkerchief, she realized she was crying and shut her laptop. Enough.

She'd be thankful to Luke for giving her a wonderful gift. For making her feel beautiful and sexy and giving her memories to look back on for the rest of her life.

That decided, she slept until the plane landed. But when she saw her mom and dad waiting for her at the airport she burst into tears again.

Partly tears of gladness. But mostly sorrow.

Okay, so, she'd need some time to work on that whole *grateful* idea.

14

Three months later

LUKE PARKED THE RENTAL at San Onofre State Beach, San Diego, and picked up the May issue of *Geographic Universe* from the passenger seat. He'd only bought the copy a week ago and already it looked ragged and thumbed through. Mainly one particular page.

She'd won.

All her dreams were coming true. If anyone deserved some happiness, it was her.

Three months since he'd seen her. And he'd never been able to get her out of his mind. He could still see the tears pooled in her eyes that last day on Maui. He'd thought then that he was too messed up for anything to ever work out between them. He'd have only dragged her down with him.

But now... Three months of outpatient therapy with the Warrior Transition Unit at Brooke Army Medical

Center. He'd made so much progress, at his psych eval-
uation two weeks ago he'd been declared stabilized.
The WTU had also helped him transition to a new spe-
cialty, and he'd been reassigned to Fort Carson, Colorado, working at Evans Army Community Hospital.
With the drawdown of troops in Afghanistan underway,
Luke had been denied his request to be reintegrated to
his unit in Kabul.

He wanted to serve honorably. But he couldn't say he
was terribly disappointed not to be back in the combat
theater. And the main reason was Kristen. Everything
he'd done would be worth it if he could convince her
to give him another chance.

It was early Saturday morning. The sun was just
edging its way above the mountains to the east. But he
remembered that she'd said she came here every Saturday morning with her dad. And he'd hoped maybe
meeting on a beach might tip things in his favor. He
only had a week before he had to report to Fort Carson.

On impulse, Luke got out of the car, pulled off his
shoes and socks and headed down to the edge of the
surf.

Unlike Hawaii, the water was icy cold, even at the
end of May. But his feet soon grew accustomed to the
temperature and he wandered down the coastline, enjoying the sand between his toes, the white triangles of
sailboats in the harbor and the purple-orange sunrise
hitting the water.

He checked his watch and it was already seven.

Damn. He didn't want to miss her. He turned and headed back up the coastline at a quick jog, back to the section of beach in front of the parking lot. The water splashed up to his T-shirt as he jogged, but he didn't care.

He looked ahead and saw a couple in black wet suits kneeling in the sand fiddling with black vests. An older man, still trim and fit, and a petite blonde.

His heart jumped and his throat swelled.

Kristen.

FROM THE CORNER OF HER EYE, Kristen saw she and her dad weren't alone on the beach anymore. Great. A jogger. Didn't they have special paths around here? And this guy was knee-deep in the surf, splashing around like a crazy person. What kind of jogger ran *in* the water?

She glanced up.

And glanced again. This time her whole body tensed, and the pain she'd worked so hard to let go of came surging back like a tidal wave, destroying months of progress in its path.

Luke.

He'd come to a halt in the water, meeting her gaze. His face and arms were tanned and his hair was shorter. The gauntness was gone from his face. He looked fit and healthy.

He strode out of the surf and headed toward her, stopping only when he was a foot away. He was barefoot, with his jeans rolled up. He looked so relaxed and at peace. His clean scent came to her on the ocean's breeze. He extended his hand to her dad. "Sir? I'm Captain Luke Andrews. Kristen and I met in Hawaii."

Her dad stood, assessing him up and down with narrowed eyes while he did so. Of course, she'd told her dad everything. Dad thought Luke was a hero for what he did that night of the crash. But he also didn't like seeing his baby girl hurting.

Finally he took Luke's hand and pumped it once. "Tom Turner."

"Mr. Turner, may I speak with your daughter in private?" Luke asked.

Her dad looked down at her, a question in his eyes.

Kristen nodded, and he cleared his throat. "I'll go get the rest of the equipment out of the car." He gave Kristen the raised-eyebrows look and then headed up to the parking lot.

The farther her dad got, the more panic settled in. Whatever Luke had to say was not going to be pleasant—was going to dredge up feelings she'd so desperately been trying to forget. She changed her mind. Wanted to call her dad back.

Luke hunkered down in front of her, his forearms on his knees. "Before you send me away, just please hear me out."

Kristen blinked back tears. She'd almost forgotten the softness and the deep timbre of his voice. She shook her head out of sheer self-preservation.

"No?" Luke asked. "Is this the same woman who

had the guts to ask a complete stranger out to dinner? And the guts to climb down a cliff to help a busload of injured people? Or how about the courage it took her to enter a profoundly personal photograph of herself in a contest?"

He knew about that? He'd seen? She sniffed and shook her head. She didn't feel like that brave woman.

"I think that's what I love about you the most. Your brave spirit."

"It is?" Wait. Did he just say *love?*

"I think I've loved you from the moment I saw you dancing in the ocean." He finally dropped his gaze. "But I was a mess, Kristen. That night of the crash. If you hadn't been there…" He shook his head. "I just froze."

Kristen wanted to tell him that was nothing to be ashamed of. But she wanted to hear what he said first.

"I did the same thing in Kabul before I went on leave," he continued. "I had to decide. Which ones can I save? Which ones are too far gone? Which ones do I let die? Who am I to decide life and death? I'm not some goddamn superhero." His voice choked on the last word.

"You're right." She couldn't stay silent anymore. "You're just a man. No one should have to make those kinds of decisions."

"I came to Maui thinking I just needed some time away. Get some sleep. Be around normal people…" He lifted his gaze back up to her. "When that didn't help, I thought I needed to let you go, for your own good. But I couldn't forget you. I knew I had to get my act together before I could be the kind of man you could love."

The sun was up now, and a couple of other early risers were making their way down to the beach. Kristen watched them for a moment. So he had mutilated her heart for her own good? Fury bubbled up and threatened to choke her.

"Should I go and let you dive?"

Yes. No. She wanted to scream at him.

She rose up on her knees and shoved him in the chest.

Eyes wide, he tumbled backward onto the sand.

"Don't you think I deserved a chance to decide for myself whether I wanted to stand by you while you became that man?" she yelled. "Did it even occur to you that I already loved you, and it was my decision?" She got to her feet and stomped down to the water, to soothe her temper and her hurt.

He came up behind her, cupped her shoulders. "I'm sorry. So sorry, Kristen. But I had to do it on my own."

She moved away from his touch, folded her arms over her chest and started walking down the beach. The waves splashed up to her calves and she dug her toes into the sand. He hadn't wanted her. It hurt, it hurt, it hurt. She couldn't stop the tears. The sun sparkling on the water seemed a mockery.

"Kristen." He caught up to her, pulled her into his arms, but she kept hers folded, a barrier between them.

His lips grazed her temple. "Is it too late for us, then? Did I screw it up so badly we can't start over?" His voice shook.

Was it? Could she forgive him for all the pain he caused and move forward? Could she trust him not to hurt her again? Now, that was a stupid question. How many times over the years had her parents fought and then decided to forgive each other and start over? No lasting relationship was ever pain free.

Of course Luke would hurt her again if they were in a relationship. And she would undoubtedly hurt him at some point, too. But, just as with her parents, if they loved each other, the good times far outweighed the bad. Together, they could work out whatever came their way. The question was, did she love him enough to go through all that pain?

"You don't have to answer right now." Luke stepped away, staring into her eyes. "I just wanted to let you know, you were right. When I got back to Fort Sam Houston, I talked to my commanding officer. I got therapy." He caught strands of her hair blowing across her face in the breeze and smoothed them behind her ear. The gesture was so familiar, her heart ached.

"I'm leaving for Colorado in a week. I've got a new assignment as a physician at the Army hospital in Colorado Springs. I know you have your new career in photography. You have the world at your fingers and I'm so proud of you."

He took her face between his hands and kissed her

softly on the lips. "I love you, Kristen." He swallowed and his jaw hitched to the left. "Maybe you could come to Colorado sometime." His hands dropped to his sides.

She saw the hope dying in his eyes, and she couldn't stand it. Who was she kidding? Absolutely, she loved him enough.

"You said you have a week before you have to leave San Diego?"

He studied her. "Yes." He said the word like a question.

"Then I guess you better come home and meet my mom and my brother, too."

Luke grinned, and it was so beautiful, his smile. "Can I take you out to dinner to celebrate you winning the contest?"

"I wouldn't have entered that photo if you hadn't suggested it. I think I should take *you* out to dinner."

His eyes shone with wetness. "As long as we're together." He took her in his arms and kissed her, his mouth desperate, hungry. His hands roamed down her body.

Her pulse sped up and her breathing shuddered. How many nights had she dreamed of being in his arms again?

"God, Kristen, I need you in my life."

Happiness radiated from her core to all points of her body. "I need you, too."

"Do you think your father would mind postponing diving today?" he mumbled between kisses.

"I think I can persuade him." She shifted her gaze up to the parking lot where her father was already waving goodbye and driving away. In fact, most of the other people on the beach were watching them.

She couldn't have cared less. She bent over and splashed him with both hands.

He sputtered. Then, with a wicked glint in his eye, he picked her up and twirled her into the surf, dipping and splashing in the cold Pacific.

Kristen screeched and laughed and then she curled her arms around his neck. "So, you dance in the ocean now?"

He kissed her lips softly and she tasted salt. "I'm just…living life to the fullest."

She threw her head back and laughed as he spun them both around. "Oh, Luke." She kissed him.

Living life to the fullest? Forever with Luke would do.

* * * * *

PASSION

COMING NEXT MONTH
AVAILABLE APRIL 10, 2012

#2149 FEELING THE HEAT
The Westmorelands
Brenda Jackson
Dr. Micah Westmoreland knows Kalina Daniels hasn't forgiven him. But he can't ignore the heat that still burns between them....

#2150 ON THE VERGE OF I DO
Dynasties: The Kincaids
Heidi Betts

#2151 HONORABLE INTENTIONS
Billionaires and Babies
Catherine Mann

#2152 WHAT LIES BENEATH
Andrea Laurence

#2153 UNFINISHED BUSINESS
Cat Schield

#2154 A BREATHLESS BRIDE
The Pearl House
Fiona Brand

REQUEST YOUR FREE BOOKS!
2 FREE NOVELS PLUS 2 FREE GIFTS!

red-hot reads!

YES! Please send me 2 FREE Harlequin® Blaze™ novels and my 2 FREE gifts (gifts are worth about $10). After receiving them, if I don't wish to receive any more books, I can return the shipping statement marked "cancel." If I don't cancel, I will receive 6 brand-new novels every month and be billed just $4.49 per book in the U.S. or $4.96 per book in Canada. That's a saving of at least 14% off the cover price. It's quite a bargain. Shipping and handling is just 50¢ per book in the U.S. and 75¢ per book in Canada.* I understand that accepting the 2 free books and gifts places me under no obligation to buy anything. I can always return a shipment and cancel at any time. Even if I never buy another book, the two free books and gifts are mine to keep forever.

151/351 HDN FEQE

Name _____
(PLEASE PRINT)

Address _____ Apt. #

City _____ State/Prov. _____ Zip/Postal Code

Signature (if under 18, a parent or guardian must sign)

Mail to the **Reader Service:**
IN U.S.A.: P.O. Box 1867, Buffalo, NY 14240-1867
IN CANADA: P.O. Box 609, Fort Erie, Ontario L2A 5X3

Not valid for current subscribers to Harlequin Blaze books.

Want to try two free books from another line?
Call 1-800-873-8635 or visit www.ReaderService.com.

* Terms and prices subject to change without notice. Prices do not include applicable taxes. Sales tax applicable in N.Y. Canadian residents will be charged applicable taxes. Offer not valid in Quebec. This offer is limited to one order per household. All orders subject to credit approval. Credit or debit balances in a customer's account(s) may be offset by any other outstanding balance owed by or to the customer. Please allow 4 to 6 weeks for delivery. Offer available while quantities last.

Your Privacy—The Reader Service is committed to protecting your privacy. Our Privacy Policy is available online at www.ReaderService.com or upon request from the Reader Service.

We make a portion of our mailing list available to reputable third parties that offer products we believe may interest you. If you prefer that we not exchange your name with third parties, or if you wish to clarify or modify your communication preferences, please visit us at www.ReaderService.com/consumerschoice or write to us at Reader Service Preference Service, P.O. Box 9062, Buffalo, NY 14269. Include your complete name and address.

HB11B

Harlequin Blaze™
red-hot reads

**Sizzling fairy tales
to make every fantasy come true!**

Fan-favorite authors
Tori Carrington and Kate Hoffmann
bring readers

Blazing Bedtime Stories, Volume VI

MAID FOR HIM...

Successful businessman Kieran Morrison doesn't dare hope for
a big catch when he goes fishing. But when he wakes up one
night to find a beautiful woman seemingly unconscious on the
deck of his sailboat, he lands one bigger than he could ever
have imagined by way of mermaid Daphne Moore.
But is she real? Or just a fantasy?

OFF THE BEATEN PATH

Greta Adler and Alex Hansen have been friends for seven years.
So when Greta agrees to accompany Alex at a mountain retreat
owned by a client, she doesn't realize that Alex has a different
path he wants their relationshiop to take.
But will Greta follow his lead?

Available April 2012 wherever books are sold.

Taft Bowman knew he'd ruined any chance he'd had for happiness with Laura Pendleton when he drove her away years ago...and into the arms of another man, thousands of miles away. Now she was back, a widow with two small children...and despite himself, he was starting to believe in second chances.

Harlequin Special® Edition® presents a new installment in USA TODAY *bestselling author RaeAnne Thayne's miniseries,* THE COWBOYS OF COLD CREEK.

Enjoy a sneak peek of A COLD CREEK REUNION

Available April 2012 from Harlequin® Special Edition®

A younger woman stood there, and from this distance he had only a strange impression, as though she was somehow standing on an island of calm amid the chaos of the scene, the flashing lights of the emergency vehicles, shouts between his crew members, the excited buzz of the crowd.

And then the woman turned and he just about tripped over a snaking fire hose somebody shouldn't have left there.

Laura.

He froze, and for the first time in fifteen years as a firefighter, he forgot about the incident, his mission, just what the hell he was doing here.

Laura.

Ten years. He hadn't seen her in all that time, since the week before their wedding when she had given him back his ring and left town. Not just town. She had left the whole damn country, as if she couldn't run far enough to get away from him.

Some part of him desperately wanted to think he had made some kind of mistake. It couldn't be her. That was just some other slender woman with a long sweep of honey-blond hair and big, blue, unforgettable eyes. But no. It was definitely Laura. Sweet and lovely.

Not his.

He was going to have to go over there and talk to her. He didn't want to. He wanted to stand there and pretend he hadn't seen her. But he was the fire chief. He couldn't hide out just because he had a painful history with the daughter of the property owner.

Sometimes he hated his job.

Will Taft and Laura be able to make the years recede...or is the gulf between them too broad to ever cross?

Find out in
A COLD CREEK REUNION
Available April 2012 from Harlequin® Special Edition®
wherever books are sold.

Celebrate the 30th anniversary
of Harlequin® Special Edition® with a bonus story
included in each Special Edition® book in April!

HSEEXP0412

ROMANTIC
SUSPENSE

Danger is hot on their heels!

Catch the thrill with author

LINDA CONRAD

Chance, Texas

Sam Chance, a U.S. marshal in the Witness Security
Service, is sworn to protect Grace Brown and her
one-year-old son after Grace testifies against an infamous
drug lord and he swears revenge. With Grace on the edge of
fleeing, Sam knows there is only one safe place he can take
her—home. But when the danger draws near, it's not just
Sam's life on the line but his heart, too.

Watch out for

Texas Baby Sanctuary

Available April 2012

Texas Manhunt

Available May 2012

Harlequin® *Romance*

Get swept away with a brand-new miniseries
by USA TODAY bestselling author

MARGARET WAY
The Langdon Dynasty

Amelia Norton knows that in order to embrace her future,
she must first face her past. As she unravels her family's secrets,
she is forced to turn to gorgeous cattleman Dev Langdon for
support—the man she vowed never to fall for again.

Against the haze of the sweltering Australian heat Mel's
guarded exterior begins to crumble...and Dev will do
whatever it takes to convince his childhood sweetheart
to be his bride.

THE CATTLE KING'S BRIDE
Available April 2012

And look for
ARGENTINIAN IN THE OUTBACK
Coming in May 2012